Groundwood Books is grateful for the opportunity to share stories and make books on the Traditional Territory of many Nations, including the Anishinabeg, the Wendat and the Haudenosaunee. It is also the Treaty Lands of the Mississaugas of the Credit. In partnership with Indigenous writers, illustrators, editors and translators, we commit to publishing stories that reflect the experiences of Indigenous Peoples. For more about our work and values, visit us at groundwoodbooks.com.

Focus. Click. Wind.

FOCUS. CLICK. WIND.

Amanda West Lewis

Groundwood Books
House of Anansi Press
Toronto / Berkeley

Published in 2023 by Groundwood Books / House of Anansi Press
groundwoodbooks.com

We gratefully acknowledge for their financial support of our publishing program the Canada Council for the Arts, the Ontario Arts Council and the Government of Canada.

With the participation of the Government of Canada
Avec la participation du gouvernement du Canada | Canada

Credits
28, 36, 201: from *The Spice Box of Earth* by Leonard Cohen, McClelland and Stewart, 1961; 35: from "Purple Haze" by Jimi Hendrix, Reprise Records, 1967; 39: from "A Tense Interlude in Hué," Catherine Leroy, *Life*, February 16, 1968; 41: from Bobby Kennedy's acceptance speech, California primary, June 5, 1968, YouTube; 80: from "Hello, I Love You" by The Doors, Elektra Records, 1968; 122-123: from *Macbeth* by William Shakespeare, The Riverside Shakespeare, Houghton Mifflin Company, 1974; 124: from *The Faerie Queene* by Edmund Spenser, 1590, Odyssey Press, 1965; 125: from "Four Strong Winds" by Ian Tyson, 1961; 127-129: from Election night coverage, CBS News, November 5, 1968, YouTube; 139, 141: from *The Wretched of the Earth* by Frantz Fanon, translated by Constance Farrington, Grove Press, 1963; 152: from "Oh, What a Beautiful Morning," *Oklahoma* by Oscar Hammerstein II, 1943; 159: from *Henry V* by William Shakespeare, The Riverside Shakespeare, Houghton Mifflin Company, 1974; 171: from "I Get Around" by Brian Wilson and Mike Love, Capitol Records, 1964; 171: from "Surfin' U.S.A." by Chuck Berry and Brian Wilson, Arc Music/Capitol Records, 1963; 177: from "Sloop John B." by The Beach Boys, Capitol Records, 1965; 182: from "Somebody to Love," by Darby Slick, recorded by Jefferson Airplane, RCA Victor, 1966; 190: from "Summertime" by Ira Gershwin and DuBose Heyward, 1935, as sung by Janis Joplin.

Library and Archives Canada Cataloguing in Publication

Title: Focus. click. wind. / Amanda West Lewis.
Names: Lewis, Amanda West, author.
Identifiers: Canadiana (print) 20220447950 | Canadiana (ebook) 20220447985 |
ISBN 9781773068992 (softcover) | ISBN 9781773069005 (EPUB)
Subjects: LCGFT: Novels.
Classification: LCC PS8623.E96448 F63 2023 | DDC jC813/.6—dc23

Cover art: photocollage and design by Michael Solomon; portrait of Catherine Leroy by Ange Zhang; "Draft Dodger" flyer from the Thomas Fisher Rare Book Library; group photo by Thaddeus Holownia, used with permission.
Design by Michael Solomon
Printed and bound in Canada

Groundwood Books is a Global Certified Accessible™ (GCA by Benetech) publisher. An ebook version of this book that meets stringent accessibility standards is available to students and readers with print disabilities.

Groundwood Books is committed to protecting our natural environment. This book is made of material from well-managed FSC®-certified forests, recycled materials and other controlled sources.

For Martha Keil

The first friend I made in Canada,
and who has been a lifeline ever since.

"If your pictures aren't good enough,
you're not close enough."

— Robert Capa

ONE

New York City
April 1968

When they come, it's the middle of the night. When they come, the barricades are no match for axes and anger. When they come, Billie is among the first to know.

She's at the window monitoring the courtyard through her camera lens when the frame is suddenly filled with police marching toward the entrance of Fayerweather Hall.

"This is it!" Dan's eyes dance. "I'm going downstairs. We'll lock arms. They'll have to drag us out."

He's at the door. She's at the door with him. She grabs his face and kisses him. Hard.

He pulls back and laughs. "Stay here. Stay with the non-resisters."

"No! I need to be there. I need to be part of it." She hears the pounding downstairs on the barricaded front door. She clicks the viewfinder closed and puts her hand on the doorknob.

He stops her. "We've been over this. You're not a Columbia student, you're underage. If there's going to be trouble, it has to be Columbia students on the front lines."

She starts to interrupt, but Dan steamrolls on.

"Stay *here,*" he repeats. "Don't resist. I don't want them messing with that beautiful face." He's out the door, racing down the stairs. "Take pictures!" he shouts over his shoulder as the door clicks shut.

She turns and looks back at the room where she has spent the past four days. Hundreds of students have occupied Columbia University, shutting down everything, and here in Fayerweather Hall there are students in every cranny, all looking rumpled from three nights of sleeping on the floor. Ashtrays overflow onto the heavy mahogany desk. Empty pizza boxes, Twinkie wrappers and stained coffee cups litter the floor.

Snap. She clicks open the viewfinder of her Rolleiflex. She turns the knob, and the dark wood of the closed door comes into focus.

She hears a wrenching sound and knows the barricades didn't hold, knows they are through the front door on the first floor.

Heavy boots pound. Heavy feet, heavy men are thundering up marble stairs.

Don't resist. Don't resist. Persuade the enemy to let you

take their picture. Catherine Leroy used that for the title of her feature in *Life* magazine. "The enemy lets me take his picture." She thinks of Leroy's steady hands on her Leica camera. The *camera* is her weapon, not her fists.

A scream. Downstairs. Where Dan is resisting arrest. Peacefully. He'd promised.

Screaming. Yelling. Words she can't make out.

Now pounding. Pounding up the stairs.

And the thick wooden door bursts open.

All she can see in her viewfinder is a mass of blue. The narrow hallway bulges with uniforms and badges. A plug of police is between her and the rest of the world. Heavy clubs are twitching.

This is the photo she wants.

Focus. Click. Wind.

"We are not resisting arrest!" someone yells. All around her, people are singing "We Shall Overcome."

Focus ...

But the blue wave crashes into the room and the first strike sends Billie spinning, careening into the others, and they all topple like bowling pins. She grabs the air as the strap on her camera breaks. Fingernails scrape her skull and force her head back. A face with snarling eyes is spitting. He's yanking, ramming her into the desk. She's crumpling, the floor is too soon, the boots gigantic in front of her.

She is not resisting! But she can't breathe, and bodies are thudding, screaming. The boot is swinging toward her face. She feels herself being pulled under the desk, warm arms holding her in a cave of safety as the world swirls and the boots move on.

And suddenly she's in a memory. She's twelve years old, under a table. There are strange men's voices, and she knows there is a gun. Her mother's strong arms are around her. Only her father's bare feet are visible. Her twelve-year-old mind didn't know what her seventeen-year-old mind now understands in this instant of memory.

A drug deal gone bad. Her mother protecting her under the table. Making them both invisible.

Become invisible under the table. Become invisible and they will go away.

Outside her memory a man screams, "We are not resisting arrest!" As though all of this is a terrible mistake.

"Resist this!" A booming voice of hatred high above her, a thud and a scream and she knows it isn't a mistake. It's a war, and she's on the losing side. Boots connect with bare legs, bodies twist into fetus shapes. She sees a rain of purple beads bounce on the plush orange carpet beside splatters of blood.

In her memory, her mother's eyes are under the table. Her mother is breathing slowly, carefully, silently. Wrapping invisibility over them both.

The heavy men stumble as they drag bare feet — the limp, not-resisting feet of thin men and women, dragged down the marble stairs.

The blue fury is spent and is receding.

And then it is silent.

In the silence, she feels the heat of the body behind her, the body with arms and fingers, the heartbeat through her backbone. The heartbeat that is not her mother's.

The silence evolves into small coughs, whimpers. She feels herself become visible under the table.

"They knew this was the nonresisters' room," the voice behind her says, lips pressed against Billie's ear. "They knew we would go quietly."

Under the desk, the arms around her unlock. Fingernails release from her skin. The body separates from her.

"You okay?"

She forces her eyes to open. She unfurls and nods, not yet sure which parts of her are not okay. She turns to look at her protector. It takes a moment to recognize her without her Coke-bottle glasses. They'd sat beside each other during the talk on Gandhi and peaceful resistance.

"Fucking pigs," says Billie.

"Fucking pigs," the girl repeats softly, blinking.

Billie looks outside of their desk cave. She stretches her arm, reaches tentatively, closes her hand on thick glasses spidered with cracks.

The girl tries to adjust the mangled form on her face. Billie looks through to the girl's kaleidoscope eyes.

"I'm sorry they got broken."

There are tentative movements in the room. She sends messages to her legs and crawls out to retrieve her camera. It looks undamaged.

Rolleiflexes are tanks, she thinks. *Good cameras for war.*

Slow-motion becomes freeze-frame. A man in a plaid shirt, blood streaming down his face, is on his knees holding a sobbing woman. Another man frowns as he tucks what's left of a torn shirt into his pants.

Purple beads and blood speckle the carpet at Billie's feet. She picks up a bead, rolls it between her fingers and puts it into her pocket. An old habit.

A filing cabinet has vomited a river of paper. Cigarette butts and paper plates are mashed into the carpet. Photos from a war zone. Quietly she focuses, clicks and winds.

The stillness in the room is strangely anticlimactic, like a play where the actors have forgotten their lines, where an audience has wandered out of the theater in the middle of a performance. She can't remember why she is there. Exhaustion seeps through her pores like a disease. Four days in the trenches of democracy has used up her store of bravery.

She wants to go home. She wants to put the skin of her old life back on and get into bed.

And when she has more energy, she wants to get these negatives developed.

First, she needs to get down the massive marble stairs. She needs to stand under the bright lights and colorful murals in the subway at 116th. She needs to sit quietly, invisibly, in the urine-drenched subway car until she can slide into the elevator at 181st and let it deliver her to the murky surface of Washington Heights.

And then she needs to sneak back into the apartment without waking up her mother.

TWO

"WHERE THE HELL HAVE YOU BEEN?"

All lights are on, blazing like midday.

"And don't bother to say Gina's. I called Gina's."

The shock of the bright lights, of her mother's anger, floods and threatens to drown her. In her mother's tight jaw the memory of a different night, a different apartment when her mother had yelled, *Where the hell have you been?* When the lights were bright, when she was barely thirteen. She'd taken money to her father. He said it was an emergency. *Bring it all. Whatever you have. Now, honey. Right now.* She'd taken the money from her mother. Not understanding he needed it for a fix. Not knowing there would be a man with a gun.

She had no idea it would be the last time she saw him.

"Gina's mother said she hasn't seen you in months. I called Dan's apartment. No answer. Where. Have. You. Been?"

Lies start to form, then dissolve. She can still feel the scrape of fingernails pulling her head back. All she's eaten today is a Danish washed down with more cups of coffee than she can remember. Her lungs ache from too many cigarettes.

"Sorry," she mutters.

"Sorry?! It's three o'clock in the morning!" Her mother's anger becomes an armored tank. "You look terrible. You smell godawful. What the hell is going on?!"

She's been in the same clothes for three days.

Will honesty earn her a bath? She raises her chin to put her mother in her sights.

"Fayerweather Hall. It was the only building we could get into."

"Where the hell is Fayerweather Hall?"

"Columbia."

"Columbia?!" Her mother's voice is rattling like shrapnel. "Columbia University?! Dan took you to the strike?"

Suddenly the past four days climb into her skin and explode out of her mouth. How dare her mother assume that going to the strike had been Dan's idea.

"THIS ISN'T ABOUT DAN! We're in the middle of a war! I had to be there!" She reaches into her bag and retrieves her camera, holding it up as proof.

"What is happening at Columbia is not a war!" Her mother's small frame is vibrating. "And you are a high-school student, and way out of your depth."

"It IS a war!" She bombards her mother with four days of consciousness-raising. "It's a war on the poor, a war on Blacks, a war on the Vietnamese and a war on every draft-age person in this country!" Her anger has revived her. "While you've been away at your conference, *I've* been learning about what is *really* going on. Do you know what Columbia is doing? They're evicting Black kids, turning them out of their homes so they can build a gym for rich White kids. Taking away their homes for a gym they can't even go to! And that's not even the worst. Did you know Columbia is getting millions of dollars from the government to make a poison they spray on the forests in Vietnam? It kills everything. Everything and everybody! Columbia is lying! The government is lying! Lying to us! All of it — lies!"

And suddenly it is no longer about Columbia or Vietnam or death of unknown thousands.

Suddenly, it's personal, it's the lie that everything would be all right.

Her mother's voice is a slow steel machete. "Do not ever lie to me again. Ever. I need you to be safe."

Five years ago, her mother had said, *I need you to be safe. You must promise never, ever to do that again.* And Billie had promised.

And her father had disappeared. They didn't know if he was alive or dead. He'd vanished without a trace. As though he'd never been there. Except for the bottomless hole he left behind. The two of them a spiraling triangle with only two points.

Her mother inhales.

"I'll run you a bath. You look terrible."

Their lives are a series of new starts that go nowhere.

All Billie has is a purple bead, a finished roll of film and a cauldron of simmering anger threatening to boil over.

THREE

She's missed only one day of school. A lifetime.

In George Washington High School she's a silverfish weaving through five thousand barracuda. When it was clear her father wasn't coming back, her mother moved them from the Lower East Side to Washington Heights. A fresh start that hasn't started. She's putting in time until her sentence is up. One more year until she leaves twelfth grade and George Washington High behind her. She hasn't bothered to make friends with the other inmates. Other than Gina.

She listens to the swish of her nylons as she navigates the polished black-and-white tiles to get to her locker. Turn to the right — 48. Two turns to the left — 32. One right — 12 —

and open. Jacket off and hung. Lunch on top shelf. Chemistry and math texts, binders, pencil case. Close and lock.

She fingers the roll of film in her sweater pocket.

By lunchtime, the ache in her body has moved to her temples. She juggles her books and her short skirt to lean over a fountain and take two aspirin.

In the cafeteria she spreads a small blue tablecloth and sets up a yellow vase with white plastic daisies. It's a ritual she started at the beginning of the year — a stage set that makes people think twice before entering. She spreads her white napkin on her lap.

"May I?" Gina asks, and Billie nods.

Gina is one of the few people at George Washington she can tolerate. Like Billie, Gina holds herself away from the tidal current. They acknowledge their shared loss — absent fathers — but they don't dwell on them.

Gina slides her tray onto the tablecloth. "You look like something the cat dragged in."

Billie shrugs, bites her sandwich. A slab of softened butter coats her mouth with sweet salt. She chews. She unscrews the lid of her thermos.

"I saw you," Gina says.

Billie's eyes flicker. Gina's eyes are watchful. "Friday. At Columbia. At the sundial."

"You were there?"

Gina nods. "My brother Lester took me. Said we were making history and that I had to be there."

"Your brother goes to Columbia?" She regrets the question immediately.

Gina snorts. "As if my brother could go to some fancy-ass White kids' college like your lame-ass boyfriend! No, the

SAS — the Student Afro-American Society, for you White girls — called folks from everywhere to support the strike, to stop Columbia from taking over Harlem Park. They needed numbers. I was a number. In Hamilton Hall."

"I was in Fayerweather," Billie says, relieved to talk. "What was it like in Hamilton? Are you okay?"

Gina tears open the mashed potato crater on her plate. Cafeteria-gray gravy escapes over a mound of cafeteria-gray peas.

"The cops came into Hamilton through an underground tunnel and asked us to leave. Politely." Gina snorts. Her voice is quiet under the clatter of cutlery. "They didn't want another Black riot on their hands. They took us out through the tunnel and then let us go."

Billie fingers her crusts. "They beat us up."

"They beat you up?" Gina looks at her steadily. "Huh. So, they beat up the White kids instead of us. Guess you took one for the team. Sorry about that."

"Why beat anyone up?"

"Why?! Jesus, Billie." Gina's whisper has turned into a hiss. "This is revolution, not a tea party. It's not gonna be pretty. They're not gonna give up without a fight."

Suddenly she sees Gina's body stiffen. A shadow falls on her sandwich.

"Where the hell were you?!"

He's spoken quietly, but the clamor of the cafeteria dims. She feels rather than hears the murmured whispers, the ripple of recognition. Dan owned this cafeteria when he was a student at George Washington, and he owns it now. She looks to Gina for a morsel of support, but Gina's face is stone.

Billie looks up at Dan. A vibrant purple bruise blurs his sharp cheekbone, spreading into a swollen and bloodshot eye. His words are distorted by a puffy lip.

"I said, where the hell were you?"

Less than twelve hours ago, her mother had asked her the same question. Was this an episode of *The Twilight Zone* — a repeated nightmare where the question is always *Where the hell were you?*

Still, she doesn't speak. When she left the campus last night, she'd wondered where *he* was and why he hadn't come to find her.

"You were supposed to let them arrest you." His eyes are cold, his jaw tight. "So, when you weren't there, with me, with the 699 other people they arrested, I was relieved. *Great*, I thought, *she'll be here soon to bail me out*. But then when you didn't come, I got worried. When they let us out of the Tombs this morning, I phoned your house but there was no answer. I went to your apartment. No Billie. I even went to St. Luke's, where they took the wounded. No Billie. I came here as a last resort, hoping I could find out where you were. And lo and behold, here you are, dining in splendor. Obviously, you are fine. Obviously, you went home to your comfy bed. Obviously, you didn't give a damn about me or anyone else. But who can blame you? Going to chemistry class is obviously more important than stopping the murder of innocent children."

The cafeteria is silent. They are center stage. The lump of sandwich has become poison in her stomach. The pain in her side throbs.

Gina stands, her chair scraping the tile floor. Her heels make her almost level with Dan. "There's no glory in being arrested, Mr. Geller. Being arrested at a protest won't change a damn thing except ease your pretty-boy White conscience."

She picks up her tray and whips away from him, but her turn is too sharp and her plate flies off the tray. Potatoes, peas and gravy arc through the air. The plate shatters at Dan's feet.

Gina doesn't skip a beat. She leans in, nose to nose with Dan. "Billie's not your piece of property. Why didn't you ask her what happened on *her* battlefield? Just because you can't see her bruises doesn't mean —"

But suddenly a swirl of girls winnows Gina out of the scene. The cheerleading team breaks through the bubble of the blue tablecloth, delicately picking their way through the mess of Gina's lunch.

"Oh, Dan, what happened to your cheek?? Are you all right?"

Gina's heels click like machine-gun fire as she exits the scene.

The blondes fawn and Billie watches as Dan becomes Dan the football hero, Dan before the Tet Offensive. Dan before he'd read *The Wretched of the Earth*. Dan before a draft that creeps closer every day.

The cheerleaders chirp.

"They arrested you? What was it like? Were you scared?"

Billie folds her white napkin carefully, so as not to make ripples in the dense fug of lust. She rolls the blue tablecloth around the vase of daisies. She squashes her uneaten crusts in the crushed paper bag, screws the lid on the thermos and replaces the cup.

Talk, laughter, banter, chatter and whispers crash against clattering dishes, slapped trays and pushed chairs, filling the space she leaves behind.

FOUR

The darkroom is her sanctuary at George Washington High. Even when she doesn't have film to develop, she goes there to think, to be alone. The art teacher, Mr. Petrie, lets her come and go, no questions asked. She has her own set of keys.

Developing film takes time and patience and discipline. The acrid smell of the chemicals, the rigorous rituals, the darkness — all give Billie a peace she can't find anywhere else. And because her father was a photographer, it is here, in the quiet of the darkroom, that she feels closest to her memories of him.

He left his Hasselblad behind. For years she thought he'd come back for it. For them. For her. For years she guarded it like a relic.

When photos started coming in from Vietnam — photos that were changing the way people thought — she started to pay attention to photojournalists. They used their cameras to tell the truth. She saw that a camera was a verb, not a noun.

When "The enemy lets me take his picture" came out in February, she saw her future. She knew what she wanted to do. Who she wanted to be. Catherine Leroy.

She still guards the Hasselblad. She's never used it. She's waiting for the right time. Waiting to see truth. For now, she's confident with the school's Rolleiflex.

She slides her key into the darkroom lock. She palms the weight of the roll of film in her pocket. She's anxious to see if the images in her mind match the reality she wants to show.

Will there be one among them that is *it*? The perfect blend of composition and meaning?

She steps into the darkroom, locks the door and turns off the light. Here in the darkroom she can make the world look the way she wants it to look.

A hint of memory tugs, distracting her.

She is bathed in red light. She is little, maybe five? She is on a high stool. There is a pinch of chemical that makes her eyes sting.

Her father's broad hands pick up a blank sheet of paper and tip it into a basin of liquid. Ripples move across the surface. There is no sound except for the whisper of the ripples.

She is still, under the red light.

And suddenly a gray smudge appears on the paper.

The smudge grows and becomes an eye.

It is magic and her father is the magician. His hands move the paper and another smudge appears and grows into a smile. A hand is holding a shell with tines like a crown, pressed to an ear.

Her ear.

Her hand, her smile, her eye. She is on the stool and she is there on the paper. Magic.

In the school's darkroom, her hands know where to find the developing canister even in the pitch dark. She pops off the lid. She takes the roll of film from her pocket and stretches the exposed tab onto the sprockets of the spool to thread it into the canister. She feels the tug as she turns the mechanism. When she hits the end, she replaces the lid and her fingers check around the canister to make sure everything is completely sealed.

Done.

She flicks on the red light. She stands over the sink and pours developing fluid into the canister, swishing it gently, keeping it in motion, covering the film evenly. She glances at the wall clock — it will take seven minutes for the developer to bring out the images on the negatives. She swims with them in a calming undersea red. She feels the sound of the liquid and her body falls into the rhythm of her hands.

Last year, Mr. Petrie made her editor of the school paper and put her in charge of taking photos for the graduation commencement. That was how Dan happened.

She knew him, of course. Star quarterback. Top marks. Valedictorian. Tawny skin that bronzed the minute the sun hit it. A chin that begged you to run your fingers along it. As close to a cliché as you could get.

It was the grad dance. He was in a white tuxedo. He'd deliberately come without a date and let it be known that he was planning on dancing with every girl.

Confidence was not a problem for Dan Geller.

He was talking to Tracy, the head cheerleader. Billie was focusing on them when suddenly he turned and walked straight up to her.

She froze. Photographers were supposed to be invisible. She felt like he'd shattered a glass wall.

"You're Billie, aren't you?" His voice was weaving a spell to paralyze her. "How come a beautiful girl like you has a boy's name?"

He'd spoken deliberately, loudly, so the entire cheerleading team would hear him. A curled lip passed down their line like shared gossip.

But her name was a red flag, and the spell he was weaving on her broke. Her mother had named her Miranda after a character in *The Tempest*. But her father had named her after the jazz singer Billie Holiday. Miranda Billie. When she and her mother moved to Washington Heights, she left Miranda behind and became Billie.

Dan had pushed her, assuming she'd melt like any other girl. But he'd pushed her right into her backbone.

"Yes, I'm Billie, after Billie Holiday. Perhaps even *you* have heard of Billie Holiday, Mr. Geller." If she had to be center stage, she was going to make it good. "And don't bother saying anything about a White girl with a Black girl's name because that will just prove how ignorant you truly are." Her legs were shaking.

"And may I enquire as to your full name, Miss Billie?"

She aimed her name at him like a loaded gun. "Miranda Billie Taylor, not at your service."

He smiled. It was a smile that said he was ready for a challenge.

He reached over and touched her camera. The shock traveled down to her navel. She flushed. She tried to move away but her groin had become liquid. He gently lifted the camera from around her neck, handed it to a minion and stretched out his hand.

"Well, Miss Miranda Billie Taylor, may I have this dance?"

It was terrifying, thrilling and completely unnerving.

"They all think they know me," he whispered as he led her onto the dance floor. "I've spent four years letting them put me in a box. Let's blow the lid off!"

He danced every dance with Billie, the invisible girl that nobody knew.

Over the summer he'd come to the Woolworth's lunch counter on 181st where she worked, bantering as she poured his coffee. When he started at Columbia, he was released from the burden of being Dan Geller, Quarterback Valedictorian. He let a beard cover the chiseled jaw and traded the muddy sweat of his football uniform for blue jeans drenched in the sweet earthy smell of marijuana. And Billie became part of his transformation.

"I've never dated a girl with brains. I'm surprised you put up with me."

Seven minutes. She drains the canister into the sink and then pours in the stop bath. Her body sways as it swishes the liquid around and around for two minutes. The images have been stopped from developing, but they need to be sealed in place.

She pours in the fixer and swirls it for five minutes. Around and around, a dance between her and the film, between her and the precious images she has sealed in the jar.

In January, on her seventeenth birthday, Dan gave her a copy of Leonard Cohen's *The Spice-Box of Earth*. He read it to her as they ate spaghetti and drank cheap strong wine. Dan's roommate Jack underscored the reading with soft chords on his guitar. It was incredibly sexy, and when they finished dinner they sailed past Jack and into Dan's bed.

Billie's not your piece of property.

Gina's statement worms itself under her skin. A line from one of the poems floats into her mind: *Who owns anything he has not made?*

Has Dan made her out of his own desire to do the unexpected?

Five minutes, and the images are set. Then ten minutes of rinsing. Mr. Petrie says five, but last summer she took a class at New School and they said ten.

The silence broken only by the gurgle of liquids.

Because of Dan, high school doesn't matter. The world matters. Together, they watch the nightly news. Together, they listen to Walter Cronkite trying to make sense of the weekly body counts in Vietnam. Together, they absorb the images of burning houses and weeping women, of bulldozers leveling lush forests, of children covered in blood and napalm burns and of men slogging through swamps with machine guns held above their heads.

Ten minutes. Rinsing done.

She inhales as she pops the lid off the canister and gently pulls away the long strip of film, holding it by the edges. She hesitates in this twilight moment, the moment before the shadows are pulled away. How much light did she capture? Did she get the speed, focus and aperture right? What does the shot reveal that her eye didn't see? Will one of the frames be the one she wants?

She exhales and flips on the overhead light.

She examines the long strip of negatives, her mind easily reversing images to make black white and white black. Three days of photographs. Three days of protests, consciousness-raising lectures, sleeping on the floor and even a wedding. The banner on Low Library. !ƧU ИIOᒐ. The Viet Cong flag and a paper bag of donuts thrown into the air to waiting protesters on the roof. The snarling jocks below. The huge poster of Malcom X flanked by men on the window ledge. A photo of Dan sleeping on the hall floor, dark curls falling like a curtain over his closed eyes.

And then the last ones. A blur of uniforms. Out-of-focus bellies protruding over shiny belt buckles. Hands clutching billy clubs. Her camera catching the moment before she is struck.

Why didn't she try to find Dan afterwards? Why didn't she look in the other rooms? She can't believe that it never occurred to her to go to the Tombs.

She picks up a clothes-peg and hangs the strip of negatives to dry.

Maybe he's still in the cafeteria. She can cut classes for the afternoon, and they can go back to her apartment. Her mother won't be home for hours.

But as she unbolts the door, clicks off the light and emerges into the world of sound, she feels the familiar tug and the edge of a cramp.

She digs into her purse for a tampon.

Forgiveness will have to wait. Dan isn't likely to forgive her without sex.

FIVE

Columbia is fading. The vibrant mauve of the bruise on her rib cage has melted into olive green. She's called Dan, but there is no answer. He hasn't called her.

She watches the news alone. CBS cameras pan lifeless, blood-splattered bodies stretched out in the streets of Saigon. North Vietnamese fighters. South Vietnamese troops. Women. Children.

Dead Americans are never shown. Only their flag-draped coffins.

In the cafeteria she eats quickly, her head down. She focuses on chewing and swallowing, her tablecloth and flowers abandoned in her locker. Her short-bitten fingernails sink into the bread in her hands.

"The strike's still on, you know."

Gina plunks her body in front of Billie. Her smile wicked, taunting.

"More schools have joined. Students in Paris are occupying a building in solidarity. Paris! The administration is starting to back down on the gym. It's working!"

Billie tries to smile but the muscles in her face seem to have atrophied, her jaw as rusty as the Tin Man's.

Gina's energy burbles over her like Glinda the Good Witch. *Come out, come out, wherever you are ...*

"I've been on breakfast duty at my little brother's school. Lester and some of the Panthers usually serve breakfasts, making sure the kids get something to eat. But with the strike, he's been on the lines at the gym site in Harlem. Everybody's pitching in."

Billie stares at the sandwich in her hand.

"Jesus, Billie. Did you hear what I said? It's working! The strike is working. What are you doing sitting here eating a tuna sandwich as though nothing is happening?! Why aren't you there?"

She mumbles into her sandwich. "I promised my mother I wouldn't go."

A beat, and Gina snatches Billie's sandwich out of her hand and grinds it into the table.

"Hey —"

"How can you eat when there's work to be done!" Gina grabs Billie's books and flies out the door of the cafeteria.

"Wait!"

Gina storms to Billie's locker.

"Open it."

I need you to be safe ...

"I can't."

"They're murdering children in Vietnam! They still might bulldoze that park! Open it!"

Billie's hands finger the combination.

Gina clatters Billie's books onto the locker floor. The photos spill and Gina's hand flashes out to grab them.

"You took these on the weekend?"

She tries to read Gina's tone. Impressed or dismissive? She nods. Gina flicks through, stopping at the blurred bellies.

"This is important. This is what you should be doing."

"I promised my mother I wouldn't go," she repeats, the words like sawdust in her mouth. "She says she needs me to be safe."

In one smooth move, Gina whisks Billie's camera off the locker shelf. She crashes the door of Billie's locker closed, spins the combination shut and turns to face her.

"No one is safe. Your mother will understand. Maybe not now, but later. You have to be there to bear witness, if nothing else." Gina is walking backwards, away from her. With her camera.

And then Gina pivots and runs with Billie's camera held high as bait, laughing as she breaks the tide of five thousand students going to classes, and Billie is racing after her across the black-and-white tiled floor, blazing down the front steps of George Washington High School, bursting from the cycle of chemistry, algebra, lunch, English and dusty ancient history and flying back into the fluorescent afternoon of life.

SIX

There are drumbeats on the sidewalk as they emerge from the subway. A wailing guitar caresses her spine.

Three days ago, the Commons was cordoned off by police. Now it's filled with hundreds of people packed onto the lawn, twined around each other, rapt attention to the band on the terrace of Ferris Booth Hall. Huge black speakers amplify subtle shifts of fingers on guitar strings.

"It's the Dead!" Gina yells above the guitars, and Billie is momentarily confused until she hears the chords and remembers. Dan's favorite band. The Grateful Dead. Gina grabs her hand and they run and she's a child, skipping, the dapple of the sunshine strobing her vision until she is pulled down into the warm mass of people.

Years of jazz clubs with her father have given her an instinct — she knows who's picking up a lead, the movement from one instrument to the next. She crouches, bringing one of the drummers into focus as he zones into a solo. She sees the rest of the world drop away from him as it drops away from her.

Focus, click, wind.

He opens the solo for the lead guitar to pick up. He supports the transition, she focuses on his sideburns.

Focus, click, wind.

A movement at the other side of the audience pulls her focus from the bass player's woven headband.

A young Black boy, no more than ten or eleven, is playing guitar on a stick. He's in the music, wailing on his imagined strings, head whirling. She ratchets up the shutter speed, leaving it slow enough to catch the blur. To catch the dancing boy, dancing to save his park.

She shifts off her knees and sits cross-legged to focus on the long fingers. And suddenly there's a face in her viewfinder, blurred and out of focus, familiar and smiling at her through her lens. *Click.* And his warm hands move the camera aside and he is there and she doesn't have time to rearrange her face and his mouth breaks her heart with its softness, his taste of cigarettes and, surprisingly, ketchup, which makes her laugh. The day becomes music and sunshine, tastes and laughter with no words spoken.

And she goes to his room as day becomes night and they start again.

❧

The ember of his cigarette is the only light in the room. It glows as he inhales and passes it to her. Jimi Hendrix howls from the record player.

You got me blowin', blowin' my mind / Is it tomorrow or just the end of time ...

"I promised my mother I wouldn't go back to Columbia."

She wants, desperately, not to care. She doesn't want to go back to her non-family and the endless cycles of guilt and anger.

Dan is lazily tracing around her nipple, pulling gently as it stiffens. He accepts the cigarette back. She tries to sound sensible.

"I can't go home. I can't bear it there anymore. This is the life I want to live. Here." She stretches her fingers along the flat of his stomach. "I can stay here with you, take photographs. Maybe sell an inside scoop to the *Times*."

He exhales smoke slowly, blowing lazy smoke rings. He pulls his arm out from under her head, rolls over and butts out the cigarette.

"You shouldn't have come here today."

"What?!" Fury explodes into her sleepy, post-sex limbs and catapults her out of his bed.

"You can't drop out of high school, Billie. You're better than that."

"What are you talking about?! You're the one who said this was more important than school!"

"It *is* important, Billie, but it isn't your fight."

"It IS my fight! I need to be here! With my camera. I can make a difference!"

"You are not the only photographer on campus. Yes." He smiles indulgently, waving away her objection. "I know you're one of the best. But that's not a good enough reason for dropping out of high school."

"Stop treating me like a child. You are not my father."

He chuckles softly and flicks back the sheet. "I think that's pretty evident." His penis stands and points directly at her like an accusation. He opens his arms, a Svengali drawing her back into his bed.

"Look." His fingers stretch to her shoulder, guiding her to his body. "It's only six weeks to the end of the year. I'll tutor you and you'll ace the exams. Then maybe in the summer we'll hitch to Frisco. You'll head back to twelfth grade with a killer tan!" His words are soft whispers, his tongue wet as it curls into her ear. "We've got to keep your old lady happy. I'll take you back tonight, smooth things out."

Light kisses patter her face, and she allows him to kiss away the hurt and betrayal.

Back on West 187th, her mother is not so easily calmed. Billie sees the crater of her own betrayal on her mother's face.

But Dan launches a preemptive strike.

"Jean, it's my fault. I took Billie to the occupation on the weekend. I was caught up in it, and thought it was an important piece of history for her to see. I had no idea it would get violent. Then when she came today, it was just to find me. Honestly, it's my fault. I should have called her. I'm really sorry."

Billie wants to scream. What is she — his private Barbie doll?

Who owns anything he has not made?

Dan turns an obsequious grin on her mother. "Jean, I know how important it is that Billie finish school and get good marks. She's promised not to cut classes again, and not to come onto the campus. I've offered to help tutor her for her exams."

She might vomit at this alliance between Dan and her mother. She wants to be treated as an equal, not as Dan's pet project. She won't give up her independence without a fight.

"What about *your* exams?" she counters. "What happens to *your* year if there are no classes at Columbia?"

"We've organized classes off campus with some of the supportive profs. My psychology class is in the Chock full o'Nuts on Amsterdam. Don't worry. It's covered. Now we just have to look after you. Okay?"

We? She wants to hit him. Hard. She looks from her boyfriend to her mother on the same side, dictating her "best interests."

All she wants is to be in control of her own life, to hold a viewfinder, focus a lens and click.

He reaches out and takes Billie's shoulders between his hands and turns her to face him. She can barely stand to look at him. Is this really the guy she's just had sex with? She can smell it on him, on her.

"I know it feels like the most important thing in the world. But you're in high school. You've got to finish." He talks quickly to keep her from interrupting. "You can work for the cause in other ways. Look, in the fall, there's going to be an election. We can't vote, but we can make sure that everyone else votes to end the war. We can work on Bobby Kennedy's campaign for president."

Billie knows Dan's playing to her mother. Her mother loves Bobby. She cried when they listened to his speech after Martin Luther King was killed. *"My brother was killed by a White man, too,"* he'd said. Bobby said it wasn't about race, it was about cowards and hate. "*We need to come together to learn how to love again.*"

But neither Billie nor Dan can vote until they are twenty-one.

"How can working on a campaign make a difference?"

"Kennedy can turn this around. He's good. Honest. He's strong on civil rights. He's as much as said he's against the war. If we can get Bobby elected, then we can have peace. Then the country can become whole again."

But Billie won't be bought so easily. "So, what? I'll knock politely on doors and tell people to please vote for Bobby Kennedy? That's how I'll make a difference?"

Dan smiles seductively. "I think if I show your photos to the Students for a Democratic Society, we can get you credentials to shoot at the Democratic rallies in the summer. Then we'll go to the Democratic convention in Chicago."

She can't stop a gasp from escaping. Her father had his Hasselblad at the Democratic convention in California in 1960. He would have gone to this one, and maybe taken her.

Can Dan actually make this happen?

Suddenly, she knows this is what she wants. She'll play by their rules if it means going to the convention.

She nods. She nods because she is seventeen, is not Catherine Leroy and can't head off on her own to Vietnam to be a war photographer. Yet.

She nods, because this might be a start.

SEVEN

Three weeks left of eleventh grade.

The Democratic primaries are coming fast and furious, but Dan says nothing more about going to the convention in August. He comes to the apartment after school, and they have just enough time for sex before her mother gets home from work. He checks her algebra, then leaves the nightly news to torment her.

Over breakfast, she rereads her *Life* magazine.

We were pedaling our rickety bicycle right into the outskirts of Hué before the bullets started popping all around and we realized just how much trouble we were in.

Catherine Leroy is out there living her life, not studying algebra. Billie promises herself that after school she'll make Dan commit to getting her to the convention.

She's finished morning toast and is painting on her eyeliner when she hears her mother scream. She's staring in the mirror when the scream turns into a sob. She's halfway down the hall when she sees her mother collapsed at the apartment door, clutching the newspaper, her legs splayed at odd angles, her tailored navy skirt bunched up, revealing a ragged garter belt.

Billie is surprised at how easily her arms stretch around her mother. They rock together briefly, until her mother releases the newspaper from her grip so that Billie can read the headline.

KENNEDY SHOT AND GRAVELY WOUNDED AFTER WINNING CALIFORNIA PRIMARY; SUSPECT SEIZED IN LOS ANGELES HOTEL; CONDITION 'STABLE' Aide Reports Senator Is 'Breathing Well' – Last Rites Given.

Billie, too, slides to the floor.

Hope has been shot. And gravely wounded.

They huddle in front of their small television, adjusting the rabbit ear antenna to make the grainy black-and-white images clearer.

The screen replays Bobby delivering his victory speech at the California primary. The screen shows cheering, a full ballroom, Bobby's blonde wife Ethel smiling shyly at his shoulder. The screen shows Bobby leaving the ballroom, walking into the back kitchen, flanked by the huge football player Rosey Grier and Ethel.

And suddenly the screen shows pandemonium, delegates, reporters, chaos as everyone tries to figure out what has happened. Shots were fired. Someone says there is blood everywhere in the back kitchen.

A young hotel busboy is interviewed, saying he put a rosary into the senator's hand. "The blood came from his hand and from his ear. I believe he was shot in the rear of the neck. I'm not sure ..."

The screen plays and replays Bobby's speech.

"I think that we can end the division within the United States ... the divisions, the violence, the disenchantment with our society ..."

The familiar gurgle of the coffee percolator punctuates the repeated loop of news coverage.

Bobby is the hope of the future. Bobby can stop the war, end the draft, make the world whole again.

We can work on Bobby Kennedy's campaign for president.

On the television, the film is only a few hours old, but the world has already gotten older. The senator is at the Good Samaritan Hospital. No one knows his condition.

A second pot of coffee swirls around the name Sirhan Sirhan, a Palestinian who hated Kennedy's support of Israel.

The air is filled with wailing. Across the street, the sidewalk spills over with people gathering in front of the synagogue.

Her mother's voice is dry from coffee and cigarettes, cigarettes and coffee.

"We're not going to overcome," she says, flicking the ashes from her cigarette into the overfull ashtray, a lumpy green ceramic cat that Billie made for her father when she was eight. Beneath the ashtray, the newspaper headlines haven't changed.

❧

Hope dies in the early hours of June 6th. By the time his death is announced, Billie, her mother and Dan have spent almost a full day staring at the television. The horror of this assassination feels apocalyptic. Billie is emotionally empty. The hole that Bobby Kennedy has left is unfathomable.

They go to the funeral at St. Patrick's Cathedral two days later, as does much of New York.

Heat radiates from the asphalt, making a shimmer on the road. Fifth Avenue is closed. The sharp sweat of thousands of bodies standing in the sun mingles with the soft sweetness of chestnut tree blossoms. Her mother's formal black hat and veil mask her tear-bloated face. Dan's thumb glides back and forth along Billie's wrist, tracing the bump of her tendon.

The streets are filled. A large man beside Billie wipes a mixture of sweat and tears from his face with a crisp cotton handkerchief. A pale boy in a small suit and a kippah holds his little sister's hand. A large woman, her hair curlers covered by a folded scarf, holds herself and dabs the corners of her eyes.

A keening moan erupts, and a woman falls to her knees, the white collar of her cobalt dress fluttering against her face as she falls, rocking and crying. Two policemen come gently to her side, murmuring softly as they lead her to sit on the curb and offer her a cup of water.

Billie frames all of these pictures in her mind. Pictures of faces that show the path of hope departing.

There is motion at the door of the cathedral, and Billie watches as six men carry the flag-draped coffin down the wide stairs one step at a time. Six men, one of them Bobby's younger brother, Teddy, who five years ago stood beside

Bobby to carry their older brother's coffin as the whole world watched.

They carry the coffin down the stairs and Fifth Avenue is silent. They carry the coffin of the man who could have been president, the dead man who could have stopped the killing. They are silently trailed by Bobby's pregnant widow, Ethel, by John's widow, Jackie, and the gray politicians — President Johnson, the Republican candidate Richard Nixon, Democratic candidates Humphrey and McGovern. One of these men will become president. But none of them will be Bobby. They are men who will mourn a fallen comrade, but they won't take up his sword.

Billie had asked Gina to come to the funeral with them. Gina snarled, "They killed King. They killed Bobby. The time for mourning and speeches is over."

Bobby's coffin is gently pushed into a black hearse. There is no hesitation as the players take their positions in designated vehicles. The procession will take the coffin to a waiting train to conduct the body to a cemetery in Washington, where he will rest beside his brother.

Billie is suddenly aware of Dan's thumb tapping on the underside of her wrist, tapping a small beat like Morse code. The hearse has left, and people are slowly peeling away like the slow rip of a bandage.

"I'm going home," her mother says dully beside her.

"We'll walk you to the subway," Dan offers.

They shuffle to 53rd Street.

"I'll see you for dinner," her mother says before being swallowed by the crowd, becoming part of the river flowing into the subway.

Dan guides her up toward Central Park. They crumple onto a bench opposite a large gold statue of General Sherman riding toward a winged woman with laurels in her hair. "Victory." Billie stares at the horse's muscled thighs.

Pigeons gather in expectation. She focuses all of her attention on the pigeons' bobbing heads. She feels as though the sound of the world has gone mute.

So she doesn't hear his first words, but knowing he has spoken, asks, "What did you say?"

"I said, I've enlisted."

She pulls her head up slowly, her eyes refocusing from the pigeons to his familiar mouth, the world spinning and only his face still.

"What?" There is a pecking at her shoe. He's spoken in Russian. The words make no sense.

"I've enlisted."

"Enlisted? In the army?"

"In the army. Yes. I tried to get into the navy, but they wouldn't take me because my marks weren't good enough, so yes, the army. It was easier."

When had he stopped holding her hand?

He offers her a cigarette. She shakes her head, watches him tear a match from the book. There's a picture of the Liberty Bell on the matchbook cover. He folds it over. *Kennedy for President, 1968* is on the back. A collector's item now.

He strikes the match into a flame, and she watches him squint as he sucks to get the cigarette lit and the smoke curls into his eyes.

"What are you talking about?"

Her voice startles the pigeons, who flutter backwards.

He responds with an inhale of smoke. She stares at his lips, which do not speak.

"You're going to Vietnam? To kill people?!"

She's standing now, facing him sitting on the bench. The smoke from his cigarette drifts past her head up into the hot blue sky. An infinite moment filled with the cooing of pigeons stretches between them until he looks up at her.

"You wouldn't understand."

He says it quietly, looking at the pigeons, flicking ash that a pigeon pecks and rejects.

"What the hell are you talking about??!!"

"You're a girl." The venom in his voice is unmistakable. "And right now you are being a stupid little girl who doesn't know shit."

Her head jerks back. "What does being a girl have to do with it?!"

"What does being a girl have to do with it?" He imitates her voice and his face contorts into a sneer. "Everything. Goddamn it, Billie. Girls don't get drafted. It's not even a question for you."

"But it isn't a question for you, either. You're in school, you've got deferment."

"I'm not going to go to school anymore. How can I, knowing that Columbia is just another part of the imperialist war machine? You heard how Columbia was paid millions — *millions* — to develop Agent Orange, and that Agent Orange poisons rivers and rice paddies and kills thousands of innocent people. The goddamned university is getting rich on it! So, no, I am not going to school anymore. They are lying bastards who can't be trusted. The whole thing is a crock. It's time to take things in our own hands."

He drops his cigarette and squishes the butt beneath his shoe. The pigeon hops two steps backwards.

"Without school, I could get called up any time."

"Then wait until you are."

"No." His voice is definite. "I'm not going to go on their agenda. I'm going willingly, now, so I'm in control. Look." He turns to her, and she sees excitement in his eyes. He takes her hand and pulls her down onto the bench beside him. "I can beat them at their own game. I've already been in touch with a couple of guys in RITA — Resistance Inside The Army. They need guys like me, guys who can subvert from the inside."

"Resistance *inside* the army? You can do that in Vietnam?"

"I won't get sent to Vietnam." He smile is broad, Dan Geller sure. "College types who volunteer get preferential treatment. I'll be an officer. In charge. Here in the United States. Subverting from the inside."

"But you'll be in charge of sending other boys to get blown up!"

"No, I can help keep them alive! I can tell them what's really going on, how they are being used by the system." He's squeezing her hands, his breath coming in short sharp gasps. "Look, if I wait around, I'll get called up, I'll get drafted and come back in a box."

"There are other choices if you get drafted. Not everybody goes."

He drops her hands and she feels the cold rush in. "Let's look long and hard at those choices, shall we? Swallow cotton balls to try to flunk my medical? A myth. Pay a doctor to say I'm a schizophrenic? Would *you* want to have that label on your record all your life? Conscientious objector status?

They wouldn't buy it from this atheist Jew. Jail? Great. Two years getting fucked up the ass."

"But you could resist. Leave the country. Go —"

"Don't say exile in Sweden or Canada! I'm not going to let them force me into some uncivilized godforsaken COLD country where you share your good times with a bunch of polar bears. Exile means never coming home again. It would kill my mother. My father would disown me. He fought in the Pacific. He's already rabbiting on about doing my duty. And, if *I* don't go, it just means they call up some poor Black kid instead. I don't want that on my conscience."

She watches him shake out another cigarette.

"Like I said, this way I'm in control. It's my decision. Not theirs." He looks at her coldly. "This way I put in my two years, and I'm out."

"But what about me? About us? You said we'd go to Frisco in the summer. And to the convention. I thought we were in this together."

"Believe it or not, this isn't about you." The match flares and lights up his eyes. "This is about me and my life." He sucks at the cigarette. "And you don't have a clue about who I am. You know one side of me. Dan Geller, the status symbol in your life. Dan Geller, who makes you feel important."

The shock unbalances her. It's a truth she doesn't want to see.

"The Dan Geller that is me, the one that *I* care about, is not going to end up in a body bag." His cold cruelty freezes her. "You of all people should understand that. You've got to take control. Lose control and you just wind up a has-been junkie like your father."

Her hand flies out and smacks his face faster than thought. Pigeons scatter in the air, startled by her violence. She's shocked herself and Dan. But the sting in her hand can't smash away the image of her father, the one that she fights against day and night. The image of her father with a needle in his arm, the image that obliterates every good memory she has.

The pigeons settle. She's left alone with General Sherman, his horse and "Victory" as Dan disappears out of the park.

EIGHT

Riots engulf the country.

She is writing her eleventh-grade exams.

She catches glimpses of Gina in the halls of George Washington, wearing a beret, her hair cropped into a short Afro. Her brother Lester walks her to and from school.

In the darkroom, Billie overexposes the photo she took of Dan sleeping on the hall floor during the strike. She watches as the chemicals make him fade. She obliterates him from the picture, as though he was never there. But as he vanishes, she wonders if maybe he is right. Maybe it is about controlling your story.

He's made a choice. Making choices keeps you in control.

She can make choices, too. She can wait for him. Fight for him. Show him she's not a stupid little girl who doesn't know shit.

Purple bell-bottoms. Rainbow-striped belt. Fitted white blouse. Hair loose. She wants to feel fresh. She wants him to feel her freshness, smell her strength.

On the oven-hot subway, she works to make her face thoughtful and mature. The kind of face that believes in making hard choices. She gets off at 114th, the stop before Columbia. She concentrates on relaxing her hands as she walks. She knocks quietly on the door.

"Not locked."

Jack is eating oatmeal from a pot balanced on the strings of his guitar. There are discordant pings with every scrape of the spoon. His free hand props open a worn copy of *The Wretched of the Earth*. As far as Billie can tell, Jack hasn't read anything else all year.

His tongue scoops back a slippery mouthful that's escaped into his beard.

"He's not here. He'll be back soon." There's a mysterious tone in his voice, the sound of expectation. "Want some oatmeal?"

She looks at the pot he's eating from and shakes her head.

"He's a selfish bastard. Don't know what you see in him." The sound of the spoon scraping the bottom of the pot is like a fingernail on a blackboard. She can tell Jack is gearing up for one of his rants. "And now he doesn't want his pretty face messed up by the revolution. He should be laying his body down for the Viet Cong, not becoming part of the murder machine."

"Dan's taking resistance into the army. And he won't have to kill anyone if he's an officer."

Jack snorts. "RITA's a joke. Once you're a part of the machine, you're killing people. Real control is saying no. Real control is taking hold of the system and breaking it." He waves his spoon at her. "You've got to say no and stop being an oppressor!"

"I'm not an oppressor."

"Don't kid yourself." Bits of oatmeal spray across the table. "Either you're on the side of the revolution or you are part of the oppressive regime." His eyes burn, and her face feels tight from the heat of his anger. "Dan should be burning his draft card and going to jail. Or building bombs."

Suddenly he smashes the pot on the table and swings the book under her nose. She's within his striking range but she wills herself not to step back.

"Seize a moment of *glory*! Do whatever it takes to end the oppression. It's time to fight back, not play it safe. It's time to bring the war home. It's time —"

"For a party?" And with that, Dan dramatically throws open the door.

"Ta-da!" With a flourish he presents one of the cheerleaders.

His face readjusts as he sees Billie.

Her eyes shift to the cheerleader. Tracy, with her cherry lipstick drawn in a perfect bow and every hair of her bleached blonde hair conforming to a perfect flip. The V-neck of her sweater frames tight skin bursting out of a push-up bra. Her face is triumphant.

Control. She will stay in control. She breathes in. She works to make Tracy invisible.

"Jack's been trying to persuade me that I am part of the oppressive regime. He says you should be burning your draft card, not enlisting. I told him you can do more for the movement from inside."

"Jack and I disagree on our methods." Dan turns from her briefly as he closes the door. When he turns back, she sees a hint of a grin at the corner of his mouth as he looks at Jack. "But we both believe in questioning authority and the rules that we've been told to play by, don't we, Jack?"

She feels an undercurrent pass between them.

"Jack, this is Tracy. Tracy, this is Jack."

All eyes are fixed on Tracy. But Jack moves around the table and puts his arm around Billie. She flinches, confused.

"I guess you two girls already know each other."

She starts to move away, but Dan reaches out and touches her face. He plays his fingers around her lips. His breath is heavy with the sweetness of marijuana.

There is no one else in the room.

"I'm sorry." She wants him to hear the words behind the words, to know that she accepts his decision.

He slides a finger into her mouth, and she closes her lips around it in a kiss. Salt and nicotine mingle on her tongue.

Dan's hand slowly slides from her face and glides down to her breast, sending an electric shock through her body.

"It was a crappy thing for me to say." His eyes never leave her face. She feels hypnotized.

But in her peripheral vision she sees Dan's left hand

reach around Tracy and stroke the nipple of her left breast.

Billie's mind splits.

"There are no rules, only the rules in your head," Jack croons as he steps in, and it becomes a choreographed dance, as his left hand moves under Billie's shirt, grazing the edge of her bra.

"We need to liberate ourselves from selfishness." Dan's voice is sure, confident, a voice of authority. "We have to remake ourselves."

Dan slides his hand under the rainbow-striped belt, his thumb caresses her navel and her stomach clenches. She sees Jack's right hand slide behind Tracy's belt while Dan's left curls into the V of Tracy's sweater.

Jack's voice is wet in her ear. "You need to open your mind, Billie. Monogamous relationships hold you back." Jack's hand slides under her bra. His finger finds her nipple. "Embrace the revolution. Make a difference and change the world."

The smell of marijuana mixes with the smell of oatmeal and Cover Girl perfume.

Dan's hand moves down to her underwear. Against her will, her body is becoming liquid.

She hears Jack's soft moan. She feels Dan press his erection-filled jeans into her side. She sees Dan's head turn and his tongue glide down Tracy's neck.

Her voice is small. "No."

She sees Tracy's eyes close and her head tip back, her mouth open in a wide smile.

And she snaps.

"No!"

She pulls them off, steps back and breaks the circle. For a moment they are suspended and framed. Until, amoeba-like, they reform and fill the space where she had been.

She is in the hall when she hears Tracy laugh.

NINE

Exams are over. School is out. She works full time at the lunch counter of Woolworth's on 181st. She buns and nets her long hair with bobby pins. She refills squat heavy coffee cups, cuts extra-large slices of banana cream pie, pockets nickel tips. But it won't be enough to get to Chicago in August.

Without Dan, without a plan, she feels cut adrift. She wants to fight. She needs to be part of the change. But she can't do it alone.

Are Jack and Dan right? Is she holding back? Will open sex bring her fully into the revolution? Has her relationship with Dan been holding her back?

In her solitude, she turns to her camera. She makes enough money to take another class at the New School. Photojournalism. She leaves the Hasselblad at home and uses the school's Rolleiflex. "Perfectly serviceable," says Mr. Reinhardt, the instructor. "If you can maneuver decent pictures out of a Rollie, you can do anything." She appreciates the challenge.

She gets darkroom access at the New School on weekends and spends hours experimenting with exposures, cropping, brightening, changing focus. The assignments are deceptively simple, and so she is deceived until she presents her results to the rest of the class and sees her work for what it is — technically competent but uninspired, completely lacking in originality.

"Stop taking pictures," Reinhardt instructs her. "Leave your camera at home. Start seeing."

And so she roams the once-familiar streets of Lower Manhattan looking at light and shadow, surfaces, angles, patterns. Streets her heart knows from childhood. Before Dan, before Vietnam.

Observe. Notice. See only what is inside a frame. Crop away the black space that tells a different story.

It's an oven-hot, late-August day at the lunch counter when she automatically turns to pour a cup of coffee for a man who has just sat down, smiling vaguely as she says, "Coffee?" She looks at the cup before looking up at the man, his freshly shaven jawline throwing his face into focus.

He grins broadly.

"Hi, Billie."

The coffee pot clangs against the lip of the cup.

"Hey, miss! Where's that BLT!?"

Her head swivels to a regular customer down the counter and she is back in the world of her work.

"Sorry. Coming right up." The BLT is waiting on the ledge of the kitchen window and her legs carry her there to pick it up. Only then does she realize she's still holding the pot of coffee. She juggles coffee and sandwich plate, knowing he's watching her. Her attention is on high alert. She forces her movements to become smooth.

She carefully places the BLT in front of the grumpy suit, refills his coffee with a bright smile and slides the ketchup closer to his side of fries.

"Can I get you anything else?"

But his mouth is already full with the crunch of lettuce and there is no choice but to walk back down to the other end of the counter, replace the coffee pot on its burner and slide a menu in front of him.

"The pie of the day is coconut cream," she says flatly.

"I've missed you."

"Miss, can I get a glass of ice water?"

"Coming right up."

Practiced movements scoop the ice, turn the tap, place the glass in front of the suit. Smile. Condensation quickly forms a ring on the counter. Her skin prickles. She thinks of Catherine Leroy ducking under the whir of helicopter blades, crouching, running with the troops. She can almost feel the vibration in the air, smell the stinging heat. She will be brave and strong.

A movement catches her eye and she sees a mother and child sit at the far end, past him, and she is flooded with relief as she walks to them, menu in hand. The child looks fierce, the mother's hair is sticking out like a dandelion head.

The menu is dismissed with a wave.

"Grilled cheese and fries. Strawberry milkshake. Two straws."

"White or brown?"

"White. Back in a minute. Bathroom." She leaves her coat draped over the stool and pulls at the boy as Billie fills out the order and hands the slip to the window. She reaches for the milkshake canister.

"Oh, miss?" His voice dripping sweet. "If you have a moment, I'd love a piece of apple pie. With ice cream."

"We're out of apple. We've got coconut cream." She reaches into the ice cream freezer to scoop out the strawberry ice cream, releasing it into the canister with a satisfying plop.

"I'll have some of that coconut cream," the suit at the far end calls out.

"Me too," he says softly.

"Coming right up," she calls to the suit.

She pours milk into the canister and sets it in the machine. With a click, dialogue is wiped out by the loud whir. She retrieves two plates, turns to the glass pie case, cuts generous portions, sets them down — one for the suit, one for him.

"I want to explain."

She turns to shut off the machine, pours the cold pink shake into the tall glass, sets it down — two straws — as the mother comes back. She smiles, delivers the grilled cheese, smiles, passes ketchup for the grilled cheese, smiles, gives the suit his bill, smiles, makes change, smiles, lifts dirty plates, pockets the dime tip from under the suit's coffee cup, smiles.

"Please." He leans forward.

"Can I get a coffee?" The harried mother lights a Camel and in her exhale looks calmer, her hair smoothed. The boy slurps the milkshake. Straws abandoned, there's a big pink mustache filling the space between lip and nose that catches Billie up. A photograph of innocence that makes her ache.

She carries the coffee pot to the woman, pours a coffee and slides the ashtray closer. She looks at the pink mustache.

Last night on the news, a Vietnamese boy about the same age was crying alone on a dirt street.

"Can I see you after work?"

He has finished his pie. She reaches for his plate and his hand grabs hers.

"Please. Just meet me after work."

She can't stop herself. She looks at him.

"Please."

His eyes. Her terms. "I've got a class tonight."

"Tomorrow? Please. We need to talk. I'm leaving for basic training next week."

His face so familiar. She wants this to be the image that loops in her mind. Incinerate the rest.

"I've got tomorrow off. I'll be at Aram's Coffee on Audubon at 184th. Ten a.m."

TEN

"What was that?!"

Under Dan's short, forced breaths, she's heard a small, metallic click. Like the sound of a key in the front door. Turning.

"Stop! I think it was the door." She whispers the words into his ear.

"It's … nothing …" he pants, hot on her face.

She freezes, and he pumps faster, harder, the smell of his sweat sharp, overpowering.

"Billie?" Her mother's voice.

"Oh, shit. Shit. Stop. Stop. STOP!"

"Huh-huh-huh-hah-ha-AH-AH." He's deaf to her panic. All of her attention is on the sounds underneath the immediate grunts in her room. She drives her mind to the hallway outside her bedroom.

"Billie?"

"AH-AH-AHHH —"

"Shhh!" she hisses in his ear. She's pinned, helpless, under the weight of his intensity. It's a force she can't stop even though her veins are ice.

"AHA-AHA-AHA-A-A-HAAA —"

"Oh, Jesus, be quiet!"

"HAA-HAA-HAAA-YEEE-YESS-AHHH-AA-GAAA-ahh-haaa —"

This isn't supposed to happen. Her mother never comes home for lunch. There's a trail of clothes like breadcrumbs leading to her bedroom. Shoes, socks, shirt, pants, underpants.

"Ahhh–haah—hannn..."

His body starts to melt.

She feels his penis slip out of her. He reaches down to pull out the safe and rolls off her.

From the living room there's a low murmur of voices.

Voices? Jerry. Of course. Her mother has come home for a matinee of her own.

If she wasn't so mortified, she'd laugh.

She hears the front door close but not slam. She feels Dan's head get heavy on her shoulder as his breath deepens.

Her mother will be surprised that they're back together. Disappointed, perhaps.

Billie squashes the small echo of disappointment in herself.

She hadn't meant to forgive him. But he'd disarmed her.

"Jack's always been into Tracy. And yeah, Tracy's always been into me. I was loosening her up to hook them up. And it worked. She's burned her bra and they're in Chicago. At the convention."

"They're in Chicago? At the convention?!"

She almost hit him again.

"Billie, I love you, you know I do."

He reached over and lifted her stiff chin, gently, tenderly. "But getting over jealousy is the first stage in true liberation. It's the first stage of being in control — of liberating ourselves from the tyranny of oppression. Monogamous relationships hold you back from new challenges and new ideas. We've got to get rid of individualism and selfishness." His speech was obviously learned at some consciousness-raising meeting.

"Screwing Tracy is part of some grand liberation plan?"

"Not Tracy specifically," he'd laughed. "Tracy's a good time — well, not that good. She's no Billie." He traced the outline of her collarbone with his pinky finger. "Look, I'm going into a celibate existence. Locked into training with a bunch of guys. I need to go with good memories." The sweetness in his face made her feel like her reaction was childish, immature. "But you? You're going to meet new people while I'm away. If you have sex with someone else, I get that. You're so great, I can't keep you to myself for always …"

Why had it sounded so sexy?

The road from Aram's to her bedroom was surprisingly short, having him in her bed too familiar.

Dan's head lifts from her shoulder. "Grab me a cigarette, babe?"

She stretches herself out of bed and follows the path of clothing to his shirt and pulls out his Lucky Strikes. She finds his pants in the living room and retrieves the lighter from his pocket. She stands naked, relaxing into post-sex, post-fear peace and clicks open the lighter. Her thumb flicks the wheel and the flame springs to life. She inhales, enjoying the tug of warmth through the tobacco. She exhales, catching her breath in her mouth to make smoke rings.

Maybe he's right. Maybe she should "liberate" herself and hop into bed with oatmeal-breath Jack while Dan is in training.

She blows another smoke ring and picks up the squashed-cat ashtray on her way back to the bedroom. As she passes him the cigarette, she sees his jaw pulled in, his eyes distant. He squints through the smoke as he takes it in.

She curls up at the other end of the bed, the blanket pulled around her, watching him.

"There's movement inside the machine, trying to break it from inside. I've got some contacts. I'm going to find out what's going on and see how to throw a wrench in the works, break it down."

She watches the smoke drift around his head, making ghostly curls in his freshly cropped hair, his smooth shaved chin. Everything in soft focus.

Instinctively she reaches for her camera. He doesn't stop her.

"But you — you've got to keep the pressure up on the outside. Jack is gonna make things happen. He's building a team. He wants you on it. The team needs a good photographer."

She zooms in. The viewfinder picks up the chain of four moles at the base of his neck. A dotted line. Cut here. Click.

She wonders if Catherine Leroy takes photographs of her lovers.

The team needs a good photographer.

ELEVEN

Her mother phones from work and asks to meet her at Childs downtown. Neutral ground.

"I assume you are being careful."

Billie raises an eyebrow.

"You're using condoms?"

"Yes, Mother."

She's finished her Salisbury steak with mushrooms, her baked potato with sour cream. She wants to be finished with this conversation.

Her mother lights a cigarette and casually blows the smoke away from the table. She catches Billie's eye.

"Do you want one?"

"Um, no. No thanks." Her mother has never offered her a cigarette. What's next? A prescription for the pill? A Scotch on the rocks?

"Do you want dessert?"

They never have dessert at home.

"I guess. Sure. Cherry cheesecake?"

Her mother waits until the waitress leaves with the order.

"We're moving," her mother announces abruptly.

Billie's head snaps up. "What?"

"We're moving," her mother repeats with finality.

"Because I'm having sex with Dan?"

"Don't be ridiculous. This has nothing to do with Dan. He's a nice boy, although I can't for the life of me figure out why he enlisted."

"A nice boy? Jesus, Mom, listen to you. Dan's a man, not a boy! A man who is trying to end this goddamned war! He's starting at Fort Devens on Monday and he's already made contact with people who are resisting inside the army."

"That's why he enlisted? That's his plan?"

"Yes! He doesn't believe in the war any more than you do! By volunteering, he'll get preferential treatment. He won't have to go over to Vietnam."

"He actually believes that?"

"It's true. He wants to be in control of the situation."

Her mother faces her full on. "No one is in control. There are no guarantees. Dan may think they won't send him, but they can, and will. You've seen the body bags. You've seen the vets coming home — shells of men with no legs, no arms, with shattered faces. Are you ready for that to be Dan?"

"That won't happen, because he isn't going over."

She reaches over and pulls a Pall Mall out of her mother's pack and lights it with a practiced air, blowing the smoke casually across the table. They tap their cigarettes against the glass ashtray, the glow burning like a slow fuse to a bomb.

Her mother stubs out her cigarette. "I've given notice on the apartment. I've found us a new place."

Billie tilts her head, eyes her mother with a thin, stiff smile. "This is my last year of high school. I'm going to buckle down, get great grades. Good enough for NYU. For the photojournalism program. I'm not going to move out of district."

Her mother pulls out a fresh cigarette. She clicks her lighter open.

"We're moving to Canada."

Billie's mouth drops open. "What?"

Her mother exhales smoke. "We're moving to Canada."

Billie feels like she has vertigo, as though she's bobbing in the middle of the ocean with no horizon to cling to. "Why on earth would we move to Canada?"

"We've got family there. My mother's just moved back from England."

"I've never even met your mother!"

"Well, now that she's back she wants to meet you." Her mother's calm voice enrages her.

"Fine, let her visit. Why should we move where she is?"

"I've been offered a job. A good job. At a publishing house in Toronto."

Billie takes a long, slow drag on her cigarette. She sets her jaw.

"Okay, you go. I'll stay. I have one more year of high school and I can look after myself. I've always looked after myself anyway."

Her mother turns a face of twisted fury at her.

"Really? And how, exactly, do you plan to do that? What do you expect to live on as you 'look after yourself'?"

Billie starts forming a plan as the words tumble out of her mouth. "I can work more hours at Woolworth's. I can work all weekend, and after school. Terry's always asking me to work more hours."

Her mother snorts. "You think you could work enough hours and go to school? Do you have any idea how expensive this city is? Even if you worked sixty hours a week, all you could afford would be a room in some flophouse. You know damned well how that would turn out."

"But I can't leave! New York is my home!"

Her mother snaps.

"Billie, wake up! This country has gone mad. When Martin Luther King was killed, the heart of the country died with him. When Bobby was shot, it proved the country is insane."

"What has that got to do with me?"

"It has everything to do with you. You talk about going to college? The strike at Columbia was just the beginning. All over the country they're throwing students in jail. The campuses are going wild and someone else is going to get shot. I'm not going to lose you to some maniac with a shotgun!"

"But ..."

"You watched the footage from the Democratic convention. You saw that NBC reporter getting slugged by a delegate on the convention floor. It was a free-for-all!"

"I don't care! I still would have gone!"

Her mother's eyes are fierce. "All the more reason I've got to get you out of here. Those 10,000 peaceful protesters were met by *35,000* armed police and National Guard! The police force were out for blood! They used so much tear gas that it seeped into the hotel rooms! You saw the protesters getting beaten up by police. You saw the blood pouring out on the steps of the convention hall. And you wanted to be there!?"

"Yes! I am part of this. I won't run away!"

"I am not running away. I'm getting us out while I still can. I'm saving your life."

"You're taking me away from everything that matters in my life!"

"No, I'm taking you to a life that matters."

"This is the life that matters! Dan is coming back on leave to see me. I can't go into exile to some igloo! I need to be here. To take photographs. I have to do this!"

"You are not going to risk your life to take pictures. I am not going to let that happen."

Her mother's voice catches. A thumbprint of pain Billie zeros in on. She knows how to wound.

"You couldn't stop him. And you can't stop me."

The table jerks and rocks unsteadily as her mother bolts up. The restaurant has become silent. Her mother's voice is a hiss. "Go to hell."

She is out the front door before Billie can catch her breath.

The stares of silent diners condemn her. Hurt and rage burrow into her like an animal.

She has never felt more alone.

The waitress slides a slice of cherry cheesecake in front of her. And the bill for the meal.

TWELVE

She's lost Round One. With no resources, her life is yanked out from under her. But her rage entrenches.

Dan had shrugged. "It's not like you can't come back whenever you want. Come back when I'm on furlough. Six months."

Jack was cheerful, helpful even. "There's a network up there. Exiles working for the movement. Make contact."

Gina was dismissive. "So you finish school in an igloo. There are worse things."

And so, she resigns herself.

She gives almost everything away. Throws her childhood into the trash. But she carefully wraps the Hasselblad in her favorite black sweater. She packs her father's portfolio, with his prints and contact sheets from the 1960 Democratic convention, the shots of John and Bobby Kennedy, then just senators, and Lyndon Johnson, who became vice-president. A moment in history that her father owned.

She vows to own her own history. Soon.

On top of the portfolio she places her copy of *Life* magazine. The faces of Viet Cong soldiers stare out from the pages. The bodies of dead American marines line the road next to bodies of Vietnamese women, men and children. Blood and grief everywhere. There's a photo of Leroy reaching for her camera, standing beside a captured US army tank. She's in a T-shirt and jeans, her blonde braid entwined in the camera straps.

A camera is a weapon. She has power in her hands.

Leroy was twenty-two when she left home for Vietnam. But Billie can't wait that long for her life to start.

She'll have to find a way to get back. On her own.

Her mother's friend Jerry has rented a small truck, more than large enough for the ten cardboard boxes, three trunks, two mattresses and one floor lamp that represent their lives.

They drive from the city, from her home, from everything she knows. She refuses to say a word. She embarks on a silence strike. Fifteen hours of aggressive silence.

In Niagara Falls they pull up to the Customs and Immigration Office. The line between her world and her exile to a vacuum.

"You've got to answer questions. Be polite. Our future depends on this."

In her mother's tension, Billie is surprised to hear fear. She wonders how far she could go to sabotage this plan.

"We're applying to be landed immigrants. Make sure you put your full name on the form."

Jerry paces outside, smoking in the fall sunshine. He doesn't need to fill out anything because he's not staying in Canada.

Through the office walls, Billie can hear the roar of the falls.

A large man sits at a tiny desk behind a Rocky Mountain range of paperwork. Her mother hands over their documents. Billie recognizes her birth certificate from the French Hospital.

"Miranda Billie?" The officer frowns at her mother. "Billie's a boy's name."

"It's her middle name. After Billie Holiday," her mother adds with the smallest of friendly smiles.

The officer stares at her blankly.

"The jazz singer?" Her mother offers the clarification as though he might have temporarily forgotten. Billie wonders if Canadians live under rocks.

The officer looks bewildered. "Isn't that a Black woman?"

"Miranda's father was a musician. He loved Billie Holiday's voice."

"Where's her father?"

Her mother looks down at her gracefully crossed hands.

"Oh." The officer clears his throat. "I'm sorry for your loss."

"Thank you." Her mother permits his misunderstanding and brings her head up to look at him directly. "My mother lives in Toronto. She's found me a job — here is the letter confirming employment — and a place for us to live. I want Miranda to have family." She looks down again. "It's been so hard."

Miranda. Billie seethes. Her mother is obviously enjoying playing the mourning widow. She wants to blurt out the truth. That her father isn't dead as far as they know. That he'd want her to stay in New York. If he knew. If he cared.

They are waved through as visitors, with the paperwork to become landed immigrants. Jean Taylor and Miranda Billie Taylor. Once they fill out the paperwork and get approved, they'll have most of the rights and responsibilities of citizenship, including health care. They just can't vote.

Not that she's old enough to vote. And besides, why would she want to vote in Canada?

Jerry pulls the truck into a driveway beside a thin gray house. He already has the back of the truck open when Billie stumbles out. The street is dark and still. Light pools on the sidewalk under streetlamps.

She peers at the house. There's a light on in the front room. Curiosity makes her break her silence strike.

"Who else lives here?"

"No one."

"We've got a whole house? Just for us?"

Her mother hands her a box. "We'll unpack in the morning. The overnight kit is in here."

She follows her mother up the path. The front door opens as they arrive on the step.

"About time. I was ready to give up on you."

An older woman with short clipped auburn hair is backlit by the hall light. Her tailored suit is immaculate. Fashionable, without being in fashion.

"It took forever to get out of the city. And we needed

to stretch at the Falls." Her mother leads the way past the woman into the hall, where she sets down her box. Billie mirrors her actions.

"Any problem at the border?"

"None. All clear. We're landed." Her mother turns to face the woman. "I'm sorry we took so long. Thank you for waiting. I appreciate it. We appreciate it."

The woman turns her steel-gray eyes on Billie, who is suddenly aware of her scraggly mess of hair, her rumpled peasant blouse, her worn jeans.

"Doris, this is Billie. Billie, this is Doris."

Doris Moore. Her grandmother.

Her experience of grandmothers is limited to picture books. This one is definitely more big bad wolf than capped granny. She sees little resemblance between this woman and her mother. Except perhaps a slight tilt of the head, and something familiar in the tightness around their mouths.

Doris's eyes haven't flickered. "She looks like Paul."

Billie straightens her spine and strides past Doris to help Jerry at the back of the truck.

Isolated words drift out with the rise and fall of her mother's voice. "Adjustment … didn't want to leave … time …"

"Can you help me with the mattresses?" Jerry asks from inside the truck. "We'll unpack the rest of the stuff tomorrow, when it's light. But we need something to sleep on tonight."

He pushes the awkward lump toward her and she grabs the handle. It's heavy and has a mind of its own, flopping to the side and sliding toward the gravel.

They walk the mattress awkwardly up the path.

"Coming through," he shouts, and Doris and her mother flatten to opposite sides of the hall. "Where do you want it?"

"Just bring it in here, in the living room. We can take it upstairs after we've had a chance to look around."

"Well, I'm off." Doris is all business. Billie knows they haven't seen each other since before she was born. "I've got to get to work early. There's milk and bread in the refrigerator, tea and coffee on the counter."

"Thank you."

"And here's the key. You'll have to get spares made." Billie watches a key drop into her mother's outstretched hand. "The phone man is coming tomorrow to get you hooked up. Give me a call when you're settled."

"Will do." Her mother leans on the front doorknob. Billie sees the tense exhaustion under her eyes.

Doris is halfway down the path when she stops and turns back. "Oh. I called about school. Jarvis Collegiate. It's the closest. There's a subway stop at Wellesley. A two-block walk. They're expecting her. She's a week late."

Billie chooses a room on the second floor at the end of the hall. There are two windows in her room. One under the eaves at the front, where dim light flickers in from the streetlamp. The other is up high at the side, overlooking the driveway and the house next door, but so high she'd have to stand on tiptoe to look out.

A Rapunzel window. With no prince in sight.

In the morning, she has no interest in helping her mother unpack.

She closes the front door with a satisfying thunk. She needs to get her bearings.

The houses on Lowther Avenue are nothing like the

brownstones in Manhattan. The front doors are all on street level, and she can't see any access to basement apartments. There is a large apartment building at the end of her street, modern and white — nothing like the square flat blocks in Washington Heights. Houses, apartments, but no people. The streets are middle-of-the-night quiet in the middle of the day. No one yells or calls or laughs. None of the slow-moving pedestrians look at her.

Maybe she's a figment of her own imagination.

A few blocks south she discovers the sprawling campus of the University of Toronto. The buildings remind her of parts of Columbia. Earnest-looking students smile sleepily at each other as they walk across a grassy common.

Her mother was right. There certainly won't be any "campus unrest" here. They'd all have to wake up first.

She weaves between residential streets and what passes for a downtown. Pawnshops, record stores, newsstands, a place called Fran's that reminds her vaguely of Childs. By mid-afternoon she's retraced her steps and finds herself on a street called Avenue Road, a name that she finds hilarious for its lack of imagination. She turns and immediately feels a change of energy. Leather-clad bikers rev noisy engines in front of narrow Victorian houses. The familiar scent of pot swirls around her. Coffee shops spill out onto the sidewalk. At one, a girl wearing go-go boots and a miniskirt dances in a cage in a second-floor window. The sound of a high male voice and a strummed guitar seep out from a dark interior.

The street sign says *Yorkville*.

It's a paint-by-numbers recreation of the Village.

Not New York, but something.

THIRTEEN

Monday. Her mother's first day at work, Billie's first day at school. The first official day of her exile. She leaves the house early, a week late, deliberately forgetting her packed tuna sandwich, deliberately wearing a very short black-and-purple check skirt and new fishnet stockings.

The subway system is a simple map of only two lines. A horizontal and a U. It's so clean that Billie wonders if they built it last week.

Jarvis Collegiate Institute looks like a huge castle. It has a parapet and a wide street in front that serves as a moat. She passes a side door flanked with students smoking and climbs the deserted front steps in full view of the troops.

Yes, the secretary in the office says, they are expecting her. Her homeroom is 12C. She is sent from the office to a "Guidance Counselor" to arrange for her courses.

"We want to make sure you are in the right courses this year, so you'll be able to take your prerequisites for university next year."

"No, I'm in twelfth grade." She can't stop her smile from being condescending. "I'll be going to university next year. In New York."

The rumpled suit folds his hands and looks at her calmly. "Actually, no. You won't have the right courses to get into any university until the end of next year. You have to finish grade thirteen."

She swallows. Hard.

"I beg your pardon?" She uses every ounce of self-control she has to stay calm. "Grade thirteen?"

Her stone features are met by Mr. Medland's potato-soft smile. "In Ontario, we give you more time to grow up before you head off to university. You don't need to be in a rush. This way, you'll be able to pull these math marks up."

She blocks out everything else he has to say. She stumbles, disoriented, into the locker-filled hall.

There's a thirteenth grade?

There's no way in hell she's staying in exile for two years.

She finds her rooms, presents teachers with a series of notes, is accepted into classes, sits at the back. All eyes swivel to her as she enters each room, then drift away as she pulls into herself and becomes an observer. She sees the swaggerers, the flirts, the clowns, the jocks, the cheerleaders, the brave poets and the intense mathematicians.

She looks for the anarchists, for someone like Gina. But it looks like all the inmates are playing by the rules.

Will they give her time off for good behavior? Or should she just make a run for it now?

She confronts a morning of French and English. She has learned about the two solitudes in Canada from her mother but can't understand the relevance of two histories.

Je serais

Tu serais

Il serait

Nous serions

Vous seriez

Ils seraient

A conditional present. Fitting.

She leaves the fortress at lunch, avoiding the fishbowl of the cafeteria. Her abandoned tuna sandwich haunts her empty stomach. She'll have to buy lunch somewhere. She finds a neighborhood diner called The Devon. She has just enough money for a plate of chips.

"You want gravy with those fries?"

"Gravy?"

"Five cents more."

"That sounds disgusting."

"Suit yourself. Vinegar?"

"What?"

"Vinegar." The waitress thrusts a glass container with a metal spigot on the end toward her. It's filled with some brown liquid.

"Do you have ketchup?"

"Ketchup? Yeah. Right here." The waitress slides the bottle toward her as she turns to the other end of the counter.

It's a dismissive gesture that Billie recognizes from her own work at Woolworth's.

"Hey." An accent that makes the word sound like *hayh*. She looks up from her chips and stares into the mirror behind the counter. Button-down collar. Trim sideburns. A forehead of pimples.

"You're new."

She avoids his eye in the mirror by looking at her fork as she spears a chip.

"How *did* you know?" She lets the sarcasm drip.

"Your accent. And your French fries. They're better with gravy."

She dips a chip into her tidy splat of ketchup, turning it artfully to coat just the right amount.

"You from the States?"

She chews slowly, carefully.

"Yeah, you must be. Only Americans eat fries with a fork." A hearty laugh. "You wanna join us? We've got a booth." A gesture. "There's a jukebox at the table. Three plays for a quarter."

She ignores him, her head down.

"There's a lot of great *mu-sic* ..." He croons the word.

She imagines spinning around and stabbing his eye with her chip-filled fork. Ketchup and blood splattering the mirror.

"Come on, everyone wants to meet you." His hand reaches for her plate, but she is faster and smashes his arm away. Their eyes lock in the mirror.

"Sheesh. Fine. Just trying to be friendly."

She feels the heat of his body leave her side and hears him return to his booth, to his friends. She focuses on her plate, on the distance her fork travels from her plate to her mouth. She hears laughter, then a song from the jukebox.

"Hello, I love you, won't you tell me your name?"

This thirteenth grade changes things. She has to get back to New York as soon as she can so she can finish high school properly.

Hello … Hello … Hello …

FOURTEEN

In her room that is not her room, she stares at the copy of *Life*. What would Catherine Leroy do?

Billie makes a list, a plan of escape, and at the top she writes:

Get a job.

She figures she'll need at least $500 to get herself settled back in New York.

Write to Dan. Write to Jack. Write to Gina.

She'll be there when Dan gets his leave. She can stay in his apartment when he goes back to training. Or she can stay with Gina.

She'll escape and go home. With her Hasselblad.

Help wanted.

She peers into the large window of a Harvey's hamburger diner.

Too close to home. Too greasy.

Help wanted.

She opens the door of the Steak n' Burger restaurant on Bloor Street. It's almost classy. The waitresses are wearing frilly white aprons and hats.

I can do this, she thinks. *Smile, get tips.* Even her mother would approve.

"We need someone for the lunch shift, during the week. Got lots of girls for weekends and night shifts."

She can't do lunch shifts during the week.

Help wanted.

The dancing girl isn't in her cage. The only music on the street comes from a guy on the corner strumming three chords repeatedly. Badly.

She walks up the steps and into the sticky dark of the house. She lets her eyes adjust. The inner walls have been taken out to turn the house into a coffee shop and bar. There are tables, about twenty. A kitchen in the back. A small stage.

A woman in bell-bottom jeans stops washing glasses.

"Not open 'til five."

"I'm here about the job."

"I don't hire kids."

Billie steps closer. She straightens her spine. She lowers her vocal register.

"I have experience. In New York."

The woman puts the glass down.

"Where you from?"

"Manhattan." Billie focuses her speech, allowing her best

Lower East Side accent to come through. She decides to let Washington Heights vanish at that moment.

"You come up with someone who's dodging?"

Billie thinks about this. It isn't exactly a lie. Her mother is fleeing the horror of the American war on itself. She nods.

"I need someone to wait tables. Friday and Saturday nights. Pay's $1.50 an hour plus a share of the tips. First set's singers, second set's strippers. You okay with strippers?"

"As long as I'm not one of them."

The woman chuckles. "Fair enough. Uniform's a bikini top and a miniskirt."

"Bikini top?"

"We've got a yellow one your size," the woman says, evaluating Billie's body.

"A yellow bikini?"

The woman laughs. "Yup. You get used to it. And it's great for tips."

What the hell, she thinks. *I need every penny I can make.*

"The clients ... sometimes they get a bit edgy. Hands on, if you know what I mean. You gotta be strong. Set your limits. Can you do that?"

A fraction of an image of Dan and Tracy and Jack flits across her mind. "Definitely."

"And you gotta watch out for the pimps and dealers. They'll offer a lot of free shit. But it's cut with stuff."

She nods. She knows how to spot dealers.

"Right. Shift's five 'til one." The woman dries her hands on a gray towel and reaches out. "Cheryl."

Billie accepts her warm grasp. "Billie."

"Cool."

❧

Two eight-hour shifts a week. Sixteen hours. $24. With tips, say $40. Depending on the split. Scrimp on everything, take lunch to school, be careful not to get runs in her stockings, give ten bucks a week to her mother to keep things sweet, the rest in her "university fund."

She can do this. She can do this! Fifteen weekends before Christmas — $450 by Christmas. She's taking back her life. She's in control.

She tells her mother about getting a job, but not about the bikini top. Or the hookers, strippers and pushers.

FIFTEEN

Dear Dan,

I'm coming home. I'm coming back at Christmas so I can finish high school at George Washington. I got a job and I'm saving up. It's at a coffee shop called Mynah Bird. I'm working Friday and Saturday nights. My uniform is a yellow bikini top and a miniskirt — use your imagination! I should get lots of tips.

I'll be at your apartment when you get leave!

Write to me as soon as you can.

Love,

Billie

P.S. Did you know that Leonard Cohen is a Canadian?

He was born in Montreal. But I think that's probably the only interesting fact about Canada.

P.P.S. Here's my address in case you lost it.

Dear Jack,

Nobody up here seems to know there's a war on. I know you gave me contacts in Montreal, but they're no good in Toronto. Toronto is 350 miles from Montreal. And in Toronto, everyone is asleep and snoring.

I've got a job and I'm saving so I can leave as soon as possible.

Are you and Tracy cool with me sleeping in Dan's room until he gets his leave?

Billie

Cheryl hands her an itsy-bitsy teeny-weeny yellow-polkadot bikini.

"Yup. Just like the song. Change in the bathroom. Wash it after your shift."

Scrawled graffiti on the mismatched walls.

Fuck the pigs

925-7210 for a blow.

She emerges with her street clothes bunched in a bundle in front of her.

"Let me see you … let me see." Cheryl grabs her clothes and shoves them in a cubby under the bar. "Good. Nice. The tips'll be great."

The doorway dims. A hulk with a ponytail and skull tattoo fills the space.

"Anyone give you a hard time, you tell me."

"Harry's got eyes in the back of his head. Smells trouble before it happens. And that includes you. Meaning don't take customers into the back for a quickie. I run a bar, not a brothel. I know the extra bucks are tempting, but you gotta decide if you're a waitress or a hooker. I see you turning tricks and you're out."

The night divides itself into Mynah Bird One and Mynah Bird Two. In Mynah Bird One she maneuvers around tables with coffee and pastries as a parade of musicians with guitars strung over bony shoulders perform to polite applause and respectful tips.

But at ten o'clock the mood changes. Piano and drums accompany strippers, who stretch out their routines to maximum effect. Coffee is replaced by beer, pastry by burgers and fries. The room heats up and Billie explores the zone where a thrust hip and friendly smile double her tips.

When she gets a five-dollar tip, she responds with a quick smile and tucks it into her bikini top.

She's at the back of the room when she realizes he's followed her. She turns and he fixes his eyes to where he knows his five is nestled between her breasts. The piano player is pulling out glissandos and the next act is gliding a scarf between her legs. The man takes a step closer, and Billie smells onions and beer. She takes a step back and he counters forward, a slow tango accented by a cymbal crash.

She's in a bikini. Not even her chewed nails are a weapon.

"You bothering my girl?"

Harry's body dwarfs the man. The sound of his cracking knuckles is like gunfire.

"Hey, man, I didn't mean nothin'," the man whines as he shrinks back to his table and puts all his attention on the stage.

"Don't make my job harder." Harry glares at her. "And that five better be in the tip bucket at the end of the night."

It is, of course. After a few weekend shifts Harry starts to trust her. The nights become a game. She and Harry do a tag team and the tips grow. During the week the prison walls of Jarvis Collegiate block her from the real world. But her weekend shifts at the Mynah Bird remind her she is alive. Remind her that she is Miranda Billie Taylor, New Yorker. Making money to go home.

Dear Gina,

Things aren't working here.

I've got a job and I'm saving everything I make so I can come back home. Can I sleep on your couch for a while? Until Dan's on leave? I need to finish twelfth grade at George Washington or I'll be stuck up here for a whole other year.

Hope your mom's all right. If things get bad for Lester tell him he can stay here. There's lots of room. Once I leave there'll be even more space.

See you in three months!

Your friend,

Billie

Billie,

You can't stay. Things are bad. The cops are beating people up for just walking on the street.

If you've got a safe house, stay there.

G.

P.S. Don't write. The Feds read the mail.

Billie's heart freezes. She needs a place to stay.

Dear Dan,

I hope you got my letter. I can't stay at Gina's and I haven't heard back from Jack yet. Maybe he and Tracy went to one of the rallies in California?

Can you phone Jack and ask if I can stay?

Love,

Billie

Weeks of empty mailboxes pass. The truth of the word *exile* hits her. "Forced removal from one's native country. Devastation. Ruin. Waste."

She has to get her life back.

SIXTEEN

They've been in the house for a month. Billie and her mother have choreographed their movements so that their pas de deux are limited to mornings in the kitchen. It's easy for them to lose each other.

There has been no sign of the gray wolf Doris. So much for family and fairy tales.

A yellow flyer floats amid morning toast and coffee cups on the wobbly picnic table. A simple line drawing of a faceless man carrying a suitcase. An appeal.

HE KNOWS THE WAR IS WRONG …
HE'S NEW IN TOWN … HE'S A
DRAFT DODGER

Open your home to an American immigrant during his first difficult days in Canada.

Billie gestures at the flyer. "What's this?"

Her mother is in her usual whirlwind of morning routine.

"It's an organization at the university that helps draft dodgers get settled." She fills her cup from the percolator on the stove. "I thought it might be something we could do. We've got so much room in the house."

Billie doesn't answer. She waits for more information. *Something we could do.* She was doing something in New York. What difference could they possibly make in no-man's-land?

"Where would they stay?"

"We can turn the dining room into a spare bedroom. We'd share the bathroom."

Billie contemplates her two slices of stale bread, the small pat of hard butter, the almost empty jar of crunchy peanut butter and the jar of strawberry jam she's just scraped clean.

"We don't have enough money to feed ourselves. How can we afford to help anyone else?"

Her mother doesn't take the bait of Billie's implied criticism. "They won't be expecting much."

The bread tears as Billie pulls the hard butter across it.

"What will they sleep on?"

"I saw some camp cots at the Sally Ann. In fairly good shape. TADP says they'll only stay for three days, just until they find a place of their own. Anyone can stand a camp cot for three days."

"TADP?"

"The Toronto Anti-Draft Program. They tell boys how to get across the border. Help them find a job, an apartment."

Billie looks up from the catastrophe that is her sandwich. "There's a whole organization doing this?"

"Several, apparently. There are a lot of boys coming across. Girls, too. Girlfriends."

She hates the way her mother calls them boys and girls. She wants to scream at her mother — *They are sweating and angry young men fighting for their lives! They are intelligent and passionate young women fighting to save their men! Ready to change the world.*

But she isn't going to take her on this morning.

She glances down at the faceless man on the flyer. "Can I keep this?"

Her mother nods. "Nothing will happen right away. Probably not until American Thanksgiving. That's when they need help."

Her mother's efficient morning routine propels her down the hall. Billie watches her peer into the mirror and reapply her lipstick.

She looks down at the flyer in her hand and turns it over.

If you weren't at the last meeting, herewith are the October 26 demonstration plans.

There's a map showing where to meet on the International Day of Protest, four days from now.

All American exiles will then be free to join whichever Canadian group they are most sympathetic to.

All American exiles.

The demonstration is at Queen's Park, about a fifteen-minute walk from her house.

SEVENTEEN

On Saturday morning, she takes out the Rolleiflex and settles it around her neck. She'd seen no reason to return it to George Washington High when they left. She can return it when she goes back.

Her hair is saturated with Mynah Bird smoke and stale beer. She didn't get to bed until after 2:00 a.m. The fall cool splashes her cheeks and wakes her up as she walks out of the house toward Bedford Road.

"Hey. You thinking about joining the camera club?"

Her head swivels like an owl's. A boy is in the driveway. About her age, but so much younger. She's seen him before, knows he lives next door, knows he goes to Jarvis. Suspects he knows she deliberately avoids him on her route to and from school.

He eyes her camera. "Tele Rolleiflex. K7S. Good. Well, serviceable, anyway."

She keeps any look of being impressed off her face. He moves in front of her.

"Seriously. You any good?"

It probably doesn't cost her anything to answer. "I try."

"You're American."

"I'm in a hurry."

She tosses the line as her feet push her forward. But he steps neatly in front of her, blocking her path.

"Clearly." He smiles in what she supposes passes for flirtatiousness in this part of the world.

"Seriously." She imitates him and maneuvers around him. "I don't have time to talk."

"Seriously," he calls, mocking. "Let me know when you're ready. I've got the keys to the school's darkroom."

She hears the jingle of keys behind her and picks up her pace. What are the chances? The Boy Next Door is in the camera club. Knows a thing or two about cameras. But by the time she reaches the walkway behind the music conservatory, she's left him far behind, physically and mentally.

The short cut, whimsically called Philosopher's Walk, will take her to the demonstration at Queen's Park. It's been five months since she was at the "peaceful" strike at Columbia. Her bruises are long gone, but the memory is vibrant. She knows how quickly a demonstration can turn. And the news footage from Chicago *was* terrifying.

But she tells herself there is no reason to be nervous. This is Canada. Land of snores.

The blue sky is a perfect backdrop for the few hardy yellow leaves clinging to the trees. She swishes through the piles of the fallen, listening to herself walking. Swish-swish. So many trees. Swish-swish.

Philosopher's Walk empties onto Harbord Street. The traffic swarming toward Queen's Park is eclectic — girls in long flowing dresses, men with long flowing hair, professor types in suede jackets, mothers with bags of toys and troops of children, serious-looking students — everyone carrying signs and laughing in the sunshine. It feels more like a party than an action to save the world. Peacefully resisting arrest won't be required.

She crosses into the egg-shaped Queen's Park. It's plunked in the middle of a circle of traffic. This tiny puddle of a park brings on a fierce longing for Central Park, for the smooth bronze mushroom of the Alice statue. For her father.

In this park the statue is a king on a horse, glorifying yet another war. Yet another leader sending troops into battle.

She feels deeply alone.

As she gets closer she sees someone has painted the horse's balls fluorescent pink. That, at least, is worth a laugh. And a shot. They'll show up, even in black and white.

Focus, click, wind. Her first photograph in Canada. Horse balls.

Blankets are stretched under the trees, and couples are wrapped around each other. Signs are propped against the huge trunks: *Make Love Not War.* The barky smell of marijuana mixes with the damp earth of fall.

People in orange robes are dancing, their shaved heads bobbing up and down, side to side in time to their tambourines. Closed eyes, beatific smiles. *Hare Krishna, Hare*

Krishna, Krishna Krishna, Hare Hare.

She sets a fast shutter speed to catch the ridiculous idea that peace will come through love. *Focus, click, wind.*

She walks south through the park and sees a knot of fifty or so people.

And suddenly, just beyond, she sees a stiff line of heavy men on heavy horses. In helmets. With clubs.

The horses are massive. Their ears are twitching on high alert.

Her heart starts to beat wildly. Suddenly, she's back in her life. When a blue wave surged into the room with clubs raised.

She lifts the Rolleiflex. She focuses her lens on the angry banners unfurled in front of the stoic horses. STOP THE IMPERIALIST WAR MACHINE! BRING THE WAR HOME! KILL THE PIGS!

Only what she sees through her lens matters. Only her hands on the dials matter. *Click.* With the camera in her hands, she knows who she is. With the camera in her hands, she's in control. *Wind.*

A cloud moves in front of the sun, and she adjusts her aperture. A man walks onto a makeshift stage with a megaphone.

She zooms in on the tension across his lip. Magnifies his clean-shaved respectability. The crowd is a backdrop, silent, waiting.

Focus.

"Canada is a good country," he begins in a midwestern American twang, "with decent-hearted people. It has a socialist base and a nonmilitaristic approach. But it has become a puppet of the United States. A combination of

British Empire colonial mentality, a lack of nationalistic feeling and a chicken-shit attitude toward business has allowed Canada to become a victim of American Vietnamization."

Click.

This is good, she thinks.

"Canadians have sold their country to the highest bidder. Americans say, Jump, and Canadians say, How high? In Vietnam, the people are fighting back. In Canada, people have rolled over and are letting themselves get fucked."

Her eyes snap to the men on horseback. Their faces are impassive. The horses do not move.

Wind.

"Ho Chi Minh is showing us how a strong nation can throw off the yokes of colonialism. We have to help Canadians see the truth of their country and to overthrow the American colonizers in Canada! Stop the Vietnamization of Canada!"

The speaker, fist raised. The calm, attentive horses beyond.

Focus. Click …

"New here?"

She looks up. A young man in a sheepskin jacket is peering earnestly at her through round owl glasses.

She winds, letting a beat pass before she says, "How can you tell?"

"You have that confused look of someone who has woken up in a foreign country where the soup of the day is always *nice.*"

She lets herself laugh, and the laugh carries a piece of who she is.

He holds out a hand.

"Martin. How long?"

"Billie. Over a month."

"Phew. I don't remember much about my first month. I had to smoke a lot of weed to dull myself down so I could function here."

"When was that?"

"A year ago. I came in the first wave. Now I'm more or less acclimatized. But I still get nostalgic when I see someone from home. You any good?"

He nods at the camera. She looks down. Did she wind that last shot?

"I'm working at it."

"You might want to be careful. Those guys on horseback aren't the only ones watching today. There are some G-men here, too. They'd be happy to take that film off your hands and use it as incriminating evidence."

"G-men?"

"FBI. They make deals with the RCMP and grab people and pull them back across the border."

"The RCMP?"

"Royal Canadian Mounted Police. Police on horses. Like these guys, but scarier. These are Toronto horse cops. Riot control, with connections. If they don't like the look of you, they hand you over to the RCMP, and the RCMP hands you over to the Feds in the States."

"They can do that?"

"Yeah. They aren't supposed to set up shop in a foreign country, but they don't see Canada that way."

The FBI are watching. The FBI are opening the mail. Nothing is ever as it seems.

"So you might want make sure you keep your camera close." She nods and closes the viewfinder. "But if you do get anything decent, we could use it for AMEX."

"AMEX?"

"The newsletter of the Union of American Exiles. I work there."

She looks up to study his face.

"Come to the UAE office when you get the film developed — 44 St. George Street. We put out a newsletter. We want to hear from people like you, people in exile who still want to make a difference."

Another speaker is on the platform. He reaches into a bag and ceremoniously puts a hat on his head. An army beret.

A rumble like the start of an avalanche vibrates around her.

People murmur, and words float up. *Baby killer. Rapist. Murderer.*

The vet clears his throat. "Yes, I am a Vietnam veteran. I am not proud that I went to war, and I am not proud that I followed orders. But I am not the enemy."

Billie's heart rate goes up. A vet. At an anti-war demonstration. A powder keg.

"No one has a better right to oppose the war than a combat GI. We've been there. We've seen the atrocities firsthand. And we *know* we have to stop this war."

Through her viewfinder she focuses on the tight jaw of a man in the crowd and leaves the vet slightly blurred.

"GIs — we've seen the war firsthand, and we're trying to stop it."

Click. Wind.

"I'm here today to tell you about something important that happened three weeks ago. Something that can change the course of the war. Private Allen Myers was facing a court-martial hearing in Fort Dix. He was being court-martialed for protesting."

Court-martialed. What does that even mean? Could Dan get into serious trouble just for protesting?

"But on October first, Private Allen Myers was given a sentence of not guilty. The verdict said that the United States Army *has* to accept a GI's right to protest. *Every* citizen has a right to protest!"

"Right on, brother!" A skinny man with an Afro like a halo pumps his fist into the air.

Billie catches the crowd's freshly cracked smiles in her viewfinder.

"GIs are putting down their guns. We're refusing to board planes. We're soldiers exercising our constitutional right to protest. And we are being heard! There is RESISTANCE INSIDE THE ARMY!"

RITA. And Dan is with them. He was right.

"This is a turning point. All across the United States, protests are being organized by active-duty GIs, reservists, Vietnam vets, and veterans of World War Two and Korea. You need to reach out and embrace the thousands of soldiers who are opposed to the war. Together, we can stop it!"

The crowd erupts in cheers.

"The armed forces are with you and we are saying, 'Hell no, we won't go!'"

The shouts drown him out. "HELL NO, WE WON'T GO! HELL NO, WE WON'T GO!" She focuses and shoots.

"HELL NO, WE WON'T GO," she shouts. "HELL NO, WE WON'T GO!"

For the first time in over a month, she feels alive.

EIGHTEEN

She bounces through her shift at the Mynah Bird, enjoying the sleekness of her skin as it brushes against strange shoulders. Tips pour in.

"What's up with you? Did you finally get laid out here in the Canadian wilderness?" Cheryl smiles wryly, and Billie responds with a noncommittal but sly shrug.

HELL NO, WE WON'T GO! carries her though a week of faded sepia days at Jarvis. Her undeveloped film is a promise burning in her pocket. She needs to see these images. But to do that, she has to get into a darkroom.

Let me know when you're ready. She's looked for him at school, but he's vanished. There's a game afoot. She balances pride with need. Her pace slows as she passes the boy's house on her way home.

But then she sees a dusty, bruised Dodge Rambler in the driveway beside her house. The back seats are piled with boxes.

She transfers her books to her hip and puts her key in the lock. The minute she opens the front door she feels the disturbance in the pattern of the house. The smell of burnt chili and something sour that she can't identify pops out at her.

Muffled sounds make her heart kick against her ribcage. She stands at the threshold, unsure. The only weapon she carries is her pencil case.

"Hello?"

A woman steps into the dusty light of the hall from the dining room. Her arms cocoon the weight of a baby, its head flopped onto her shoulder.

"Oh, hi. Y'all must be Billie," she says softly. "I'm Linda."

Billie vaguely remembers her mother saying something about a dodger coming to stay with them. Had she said something about a woman and a baby?

"I'm just tryin' to get this little guy to sleep. He picked up a cold somewheres on the road, and he's been quite a grumpy puss."

Billie slowly closes the front door. Her heartbeat slows and her eyes adjust to the dim light. She can see beyond the woman into the kitchen. Their kitchen picnic table is scattered with dirty dishes.

"Your momma came home from work to let us in. She couldn't stay long. Said we could help ourselves to some of your excellent chili. We been livin' on popcorn and Kool-Aid since we left home, so that chili sure did taste sweet."

"Popcorn and Kool-Aid?"

"Popcorn and Kool-Aid's about the cheapest thing you can fill your tummy with." Linda jiggled the baby gently. "We didn't have much money saved before we left."

Billie finally moves her legs. She dumps her books on the hall table. Linda and the baby slide softly out of her way as she heads toward the kitchen.

"How long have you been on the road?"

"Took us two days to drive here from Tuscaloosa. We weren't sure we were gonna leave. When Kenny got his notice, he went for the inspection and all and then he got told to report in seven days. We had to decide pretty fast. He was willing to go, but I just looked at little Joey here and said I didn't want him to grow up without a daddy. My momma, she cried and begged us not to go. My papa, he wouldn't even talk to Kenny. And we didn't tell Kenny's folks on account of they might have reported him and they would've thrown him in jail at the border. I can tell you, we were pretty nervous when we were crossin'. We were waitin' for them to nab us right there and then." Linda allows a soft, sad laugh to escape as she jiggles the baby up and down. "I can hardly believe we made it."

Billie automatically fills the sink. The warm soapy water soothes her hands and calms her mind. She gathers up the bowls and spoons from the table. A quick glance at the chili pot. Half gone.

She hadn't bargained on this. She had imagined a young man like Dan needing care and support, not this chatty young mother, barely older than herself, filling the corners of the house with her life story.

She plunges her hands deeper into the water as the baby starts to cry in earnest.

Something we could do.

Feeding chili to Southern mommas is not how you start a revolution.

But she has a roll of film. Waiting to be developed.

NINETEEN

"Can you get me into the darkroom?"

Scott turns slowly to face her with a self-satisfied smile. "Well, hello. Nice to see you, too."

The subway platform is full of commuters but empty of life. Toronto subways are squeaky clean — not a rat or a cockroach to be seen. No one vomiting on the tracks. No one singing, no one shouting.

"Okay, yeah, hello. I want to use the school's darkroom."

"Do you know how?"

She stops herself from snapping. "They gave me free rein at the New School." No reaction. She bristles. "It's an art college. In Manhattan."

He looks at her. "I've heard of it. So I'm supposed to kiss the ground beneath your feet?"

Status ignored is always higher status. Touché.

"It would be a start." She turns to face the tunnel as the distant rumble moves up through her feet.

"Scott."

She waits a beat. Looks at him.

"Scott McGregor."

"Billie. Billie Taylor. Well, can I?"

"I told you, I've got the keys. I'm the president of the camera club."

If he is waiting for a reaction, she'll disappoint him.

"When?"

"Lunch."

The door stops in front of them and a mass of university students overflows onto the platform. She deftly sidesteps to the waiting commuters at the next car over, separating herself from him.

As the train pulls out of the station, she sees him standing on the platform. Saluting.

Two minutes after the lunch bell rings she is striding down the hall toward the darkroom. She fingers the hard roll of film. Precious cargo. She assumes she'll get there first, but he is waiting with a fresh salute and a wry smile.

"M'lady."

"Yeah. Thanks so much. Really appreciate this." She holds her hand out for the keys.

"Whoa, sugar plum. This is my castle and I'm responsible for what happens here. You'll have to prove you know your stuff. So I'll be in there with you."

Her patience snaps.

"Look, I don't need this crap. I'm trying to get my prints developed, not have a quickie over lunch. I'm actually serious about this stuff, and I'm not going to trade darkroom privileges for sexual favors."

His eyes turn steely gray. His voice is cold.

"If it is possible for you to get off your American high horse, we can get down to developing your film. You're not an official member of the camera club, and until you are, you play by my rules."

In his anger she recognizes someone who cares as much about cameras as she does.

He pushes open the outer door. The "Dark Room in Use" light is off.

She's washed with familiar smells — the pinch of chemicals, of body odor, of stale cigarettes. Possibly beer. The longing for her darkroom at George Washington High smacks her like a knockout round.

"Welcome to my kingdom, princess." He reaches for a pack of Rothmans and offers one.

"After?" She wants to get down to business.

"Sure thing."

Her eyes flit around the room. There's a sink and a large washtub with hoses in and out. Clotheslines crisscross the space. It's tidy and well managed. He turns on a fan and leans back against the sink.

"Take what you need."

And so she does, methodically assembling equipment on the counter. The chemicals are all in jars in a tidy row. Dektol developing fluid. Stop bath. Fixer.

"Filtered?" She gestures to the water jug and he nods. She tests the temperature and mixes the proportions without looking at the charts on the walls, too focused to care if she's impressing him. She finds the developing canister, takes her film from her pocket and sets everything in order.

She's aware of him, smoking and watching.

"Okay. I'm ready."

He turns on the tap to douse his cigarette. He switches on the outer red light and locks the inner door.

He turns off the light and they are plunged into complete darkness.

She breathes slowly as her eyes and ears adjust. She listens for any movement on his side of the room. She doesn't trust him entirely, but she needs to stay on his good side, needs to prove she knows what she is doing, needs the keys to this particular castle. If groping in the dark is the price, she might have to put up with it.

But the darkness is filled only with the smell of the open can of stop bath. Her hands move blindly through the sequence. Film threaded and spiraled into the developing canister. The click of the lid is like a shotgun in the silence.

He flicks on the red work light, knowing that she is ready. She wonders briefly how he knows she prefers to work out of the glare of the incandescent. The swish of the liquid soothes her and makes her forget about him again. She can't stop her body swaying as her hands cradle the canister and the liquid coats the hidden film.

She moves through the choreography of developing fluid, stop bath, fixer and rinsing. She watches the wall clock and feels his tension as she stretches the rinsing to seven minutes.

The lid pops off with a sucking noise. Her fingers search for the edges of the film.

"You ready for the light?"

He's read her mind and she nods, anxious in this moment of anticipation. She inhales, not wanting him to feel anything of what she feels.

He switches on the dim light.

Her breath catches.

Dan. Dan, all black and smooth in the negative where light is dark and dark is light. Dan, that last day in her bed, leaning back on her pillows, chest bare, smoking, like something in an Italian movie.

Her bed. Her home. A negative of home. It threatens to undo her.

All she wants right now is to look at Dan, but not in front of Scott.

The negatives leap from Dan to the demonstration. Nothing in between. From home to exile. She scans quickly. She's desperate to see something good that she can give AMEX, something they might publish. But there's nothing special.

Until … there. There it is. The vet, the hippies and the horses. All in one. Hope, anger, fear, coiled anticipation. The edge of violence. Everything. It's a photo she can take to Martin. And send to Jack.

They need a good photographer.

She picks up a clothes-peg and carefully hangs the long strip on the line.

"You want that smoke?"

She's startled. She forgot he was here, watching her.

"Yes. Thank you."

He offers her the pack and then clicks open his lighter to

light hers, and then his. She enjoys a luxurious exhale.

"Was it good for you?" His languid voice momentarily confuses her until he blows out smoke exaggeratedly and she chokes on her lungful and laughs.

"You're hateful."

"Yes, I know."

"Do I get the keys?"

"No." She starts to object. "Not yet. You've got to play by the same rules as everyone else, Princess New York. I'll meet you here tomorrow, same time, same place, to make the prints."

A distant bell rings.

"And that, m'lady, is the end of lunch period. You might want to hustle so you don't have to deal with late slips."

"What about you?"

"I never go to class. I tell them I am taking photos for the yearbook. I'll probably fail my year, but frankly, Scarlett, I don't give a damn. You, however, might not want to draw attention to yourself, and since I can't grant you immunity, I'd suggest you get a move on."

She exhales and douses her cigarette with water before dropping it in the trash. She takes a quick glance at the long curl of film hanging from the line.

"Don't worry. Your secrets are safe with me."

She knows he'll look at them.

She hopes the picture of Dan shocks him. She hopes it makes him realize she's out of his league.

She hopes it impresses him enough to give her the keys. Soon.

TWENTY

"It's near a place called High Park. Third floor of a house. Lots of stairs, but real pretty. Room for Joey to play. And Kenny's got a job at a garage nearby, don't you, honey? They said they were real happy to have him. Happy to have a family man, they said."

Linda is shoving baby toys and blankets into her big bag. Billie hadn't expected them to leave so soon. Her mother isn't home from work, and she feels as though she should be signing them out or something.

"Honey, I know you're real serious about your camera, so I'm wondering if y'all would take a photograph of us. To send to my momma?"

Kenny stops mid-trip to the car, a garbage bag of clothes in his arms. "I don't know, Linda. Might not be such a good idea."

"Kenny, I gotta let them know we're okay."

"But what if the FBI come lookin' an' buggin' your folks? They can't know where we are."

Linda shifts Joey to her hip and takes the bag of clothes out of Kenny's arms.

"You'll just take it and send it, won't ya, honey? No return address. Just send it to my momma?" She grabs Billie's school binder, finds a blank page and scribbles an address in Alabama, all the while tilting her head so Joey can play with her ponytail.

"I'm not that good at portraits." Truth is, she isn't sure how long her darkroom privileges will last. She doesn't want to waste one precious moment on a family portrait. She has to pay for the film and paper. Money that comes out of her escape fund.

"Please, honey? You been so good to us. I know if it was you, your momma would sure want to know you were okay."

If we were a real family, Billie thinks.

But she knows they won't go until she does this, so she sets the little family in front of the fireplace. She scans the background to make sure there is nothing identifiable. Nothing the FBI could trace. *It could be any fireplace in any old house,* she thinks.

Joey squirms in Linda's arms, so she sets a fast speed in case he moves when she shoots. Billie calls out for his attention.

"Hey, Joey!"

And he turns his head to find her and in that moment there's a click and they are captured.

There's an immediate exhale and a frenzy of movement, as though they've been released from a block of ice.

"I'll let you know when we're settled. You'll come visit us, won't ya now?" She gives a small giggle and coos into Joey's ear. "We're gonna miss Miss Billie, aren't we, sweetie pie?"

She leans over so that Billie can — what? Take him, hug him, kiss him? She hates babies. But Joey solves the awkwardness by grabbing his mother's neck and burying his face in her hair.

"Oh, you tinker. Playin' strange." The love beams out of Linda and coats the baby.

"Come *on*, Linda." Kenny scoops up their coats and heads to the car.

Linda the whirlwind grabs the bag of baby supplies.

"You look after yourself, Miss Billie. An' thank your momma for us. I don't know what we woulda done without y'all."

Billie watches the car pull out of the driveway, head down the block and turn the corner. A cyclone whirling into the distance.

"Alabama's gone?" Scott is standing at his front door.

She nods.

"Back to an empty house?"

She shrugs.

"Lunch tomorrow?"

She thinks of her negatives hanging there, waiting.

"Unless I get a better offer," she says as she strides off stage to a kitchen filled with the stench of dirty diapers, and the vague sense that this boy next door is the closest thing she has to a friend.

TWENTY-ONE

She prints five of the demonstration photos for Martin. She has to get them to him by the end of the week if she has any hope of getting one in the newsletter. She'll make duplicates for Jack. But she's not sure how she'll send them.

The Feds read the mail.

She knows Scott's impressed by the prints.

"Boyfriend?" He nods at the photo of Dan. Enlarged, it's striking. She caught the smoke coddling his cheekbone, his squinting eye giving him the rakish look of a pirate.

She nods. "He got drafted." It's easier than the truth.

"That sucks. I can't imagine it."

"Which part?"

"All of it. Getting drafted. Going to the other side of the world to kill people. Maybe getting killed yourself. I mean, what's it all for? I sure wouldn't go."

"Oh, really? Really. Has it never occurred to you that you might not have a choice?"

"Oh, come on, you always have a choice."

"No, you don't. If they draft you, you have to go. Or they throw you in jail."

"I'd tell them it was against my religion."

"You'd have to prove it. They'd still put you in jail. Or make you do two years of community service, which is almost the same thing."

"Well, I'd fight that."

"Yeah, big shot, that's what protests are."

"But what's the point of protesting? This picture you took …" He holds up the photo of the vet, the horses. "They're all Americans, right?"

"Yes."

"Why are they protesting here? Canada's got nothing to do with the war."

"Oh, god, are all Canadians so stupid? Don't you realize that Canada is part of the imperialist war machine that is slaughtering millions of innocent people?" He squints at her incredulously. "You really don't get it, do you? If you aren't part of the solution, you're part of the problem."

"And you think these protests are part of the solution?" His voice tries to be condescending, but all she can do is laugh. His naivety goads her.

"Yes. Yes, I do." The war is dragging on. The body counts

are piling up. Anger curls her fist. "I'm at least trying to be part of the solution. What the hell are you doing?"

She grabs up her contact sheets and prints and pushes past him out of the darkroom. She decides to cut classes for the rest of the day and head straight to the Union of American Exiles.

The office of the Union of American Exiles at 44 St. George Street is not what she was expecting. A mansion. Big, turreted, red brick with bay windows. She's sure she has the wrong address, but the name Union of American Exiles is on the mailbox outside, along with the U of T Student Movement, the Women's Liberation Front and the Student Labour Committee.

Pretty posh accommodations for an insurrection, she thinks.

The UAE office is in the basement. The staircase curves down to an open room filled with a desk, couch, stacks of books, coffee cups, overfilled ashtrays and, in the corner, a beat-up Gestetner machine.

Billie's eyes bounce off scribbled signs papering the grimy walls:

You've got to put your bodies upon the gears and upon the wheels, upon the levers, upon all the apparatus, and you've got to make it stop. — Mario Savio

We revolt simply because, for many reasons, we can no longer breathe. — Frantz Fanon

We cannot be sure of having something to live for unless we are willing to die for it. — Che Guevara

"Yeah?"

Martin peers at her from over the typewriter, glasses pushed back into his thick curls. He looks like he hasn't slept since she saw him. She's pretty sure he's wearing the same clothes.

"Hi." She's suddenly nervous. She knows the photos are good, but maybe they aren't good enough. "We met the other day. At the demonstration?"

He pulls down his glasses and stares at her.

"The chick with the camera."

She nods.

"Did you get anything decent?"

"Maybe."

"Great! Let's take a look." He bounds up from the wooden swivel chair and steers her toward the other side of the room, to a large flat table made from a door. There's a cutting board covered in staples scattered like birdseed.

She hands him the envelope of five prints. She's curious to see if he can pick out the best, the one with the vet, or if he'll just see them as snaps and take the one with the best crowd picture.

He scatters them on the table in a manner that is both casual and professional. "Getting good photos is hard. Nobody's got a camera anymore. They all got sold for rent."

She's bridles at the implication that if she was really fighting for the cause, she would be poorer than she is and have sold her camera.

"I took it from my last school. In New York."

"Nice." The implication of theft seems to impress him.

He spreads the prints out.

"Not bad. Yeah, really, not bad. Oh, this one is great.

We could use this."

He lifts up the one with the vet.

She isn't sure if taking pride in the work is appropriate or too bourgeois. So she just nods.

"I've got a copy of the guy's speech." His eyes drill into the photo, as though it is bringing the moment back. "Not something you hear very often. A vet against the war."

"Apparently there are quite a few."

He turns to her, his face a question mark.

She hesitates. "My boyfriend. He's working with RITA. Trying to do what he can from the inside."

"Where is he?"

"Fort Devens."

"He didn't dodge?"

"He enlisted so he wouldn't get sent over. So he could stay in control and organize the resistance."

Martin leans back against the table and crosses his arms. When he finally speaks, his voice is thick with anger.

"A lot of guys fall for that line."

"Dan knows what he's doing."

"I hope so, for his sake." He turns around, picks up a package of Craven A cigarettes and offers one to Billie. "The training changes you …" He flips his lighter and lights hers before leaning down to light his own.

She blows out the smoke and looks down at the print.

"It's good enough? You'll print it?"

"Yeah, it's great. Love it. We'll put it in the next issue. You want a line credit, or you want to be anonymous?"

She frowns. "Anonymous?"

"Some folks don't want their names associated with a radical paper. The Feds pick on guys with radical backgrounds.

Send them up first if they're in the States. Start tailing them in Canada. But you're a girl. It's probably okay. So, what do we put?"

Her first official byline. A photo that can make a difference. Not one her father would ever see, but she wants her name on it, in case. His part of her name.

"Billie Taylor. Billie with an I E. As in Holiday. Taylor with a Y."

"Cool." He writes it on the back of the print. "Hey, are you related to Mrs. Taylor, the one on Lowther Avenue?"

"She's my mom."

"Cool! You guys are on the Underground Railroad list. You're mom's pretty hip about it all."

She gives a shrug. "Trying to do our part."

"That's so cool. I wish my mom understood any of this. She stopped speaking to me the day I left."

"Dodger?"

"Deserter."

The word carries a story-sized pause. Deserting is a federal offense. It used to be punishable by death. She can see him watching for her reaction.

She nods. She admires his guts. The weight of the pause sits between them.

She sees him come to a decision. "Listen, we're having an election party Tuesday night. Going to watch the returns at Rochdale. Why don't you come?"

Her mother is expecting to watch the returns with her. She's already bought the snacks.

"Sounds great." She means it.

"Cool. Meet me in the Rochdale lobby at seven. We'll have popcorn and beer, some weed."

Martin puts her photos back in the envelope, except for the one with the vet, which he places carefully on his desk.

"I turned twenty-one the day before they shot Bobby. This would have been my first election, the first time I could have voted. But now I don't think change will happen in the ballot box."

He holds her eyes a bit too long. "We have to take responsibility. We have to take control."

He nods. She nods. She feels she's passed some test.

"Tuesday. The Rochdale lobby." He sets up the print on his desk. "Damn, that's a good photo."

Again, that open smile. She feels like she hasn't seen a real smile since she crossed the border.

"But don't bring your camera. There are people who need to stay invisible."

TWENTY-TWO

Halloween brings an assortment of ghosts, monsters and witches to their door to receive caramel toffee kisses and apples. One young blonde witch with a makeup wart on her nose and teeth blacked out with wax recites the witches' speech from *Macbeth*.

Double, double, toil and trouble
Fire burn and cauldron bubble …

The words stick in Billie's head. It's a play she studied at George Washingtoon High. Armed with leftover candy, she spends the weekend reading. Her father gave her a complete edition of Shakespeare for her tenth birthday. Now, one line from Lady Macduff confronts her.

When our actions do not, our fears do make us traitors.

Every day, her inaction makes her a traitor. A traitor to Dan, to Jack, to the people of Vietnam, to herself. Her inability to do the simplest thing — to vote — infuriates her. Although with only Humphrey, Nixon and the segregationist Wallace on the ticket, it's hard to see how any of it will make a difference.

The election is not front-page news in Canada. No one even mentions it at school. Going to Rochdale means she'll be with people who care, who know this election matters.

She dresses thoughtfully. A serious photographer who has left her camera at home. A politically savvy American. She trades the rainbow belt on her bell-bottoms for a plain wide white one. Her favorite black sweater is a bit too tight over her breasts, but it is better than anything with color.

Downstairs in their living room, the TV is already on. Her mother has settled in for a long night with a Bloody Mary and a bowl of pretzels. She turns her head from the screen to see Billie putting on her coat.

"You're going out?'

Every word an accusation. Billie's rage a permanent dull simmer.

"Yeah, I'm going to watch the returns with some friends."

"I thought we were going to watch together."

Billie doesn't bite. "I'm watching at Rochdale."

Her mother's jaw tightens. She turns her head back to their tiny TV.

Billie yanks open the front door. It's not her problem that her mother has a small life in a large empty house. The fall air goes straight to her bloodstream as her long strides increase the distance between them.

Rochdale: Canada's first free university. The building is just off the U of T campus, only five blocks from their house. Her mother told her about it, maybe thinking she was dangling a carrot to make up for the crisis of the thirteenth grade. Billie admits that it sounds pretty good — students take whatever subjects they want and find their own teachers. The apartment building is part dormitory, part cheap housing, part college with seminar rooms. If they had a decent photography school, she might have looked into it. Except that it's in Toronto and she isn't staying so it doesn't matter. By January she'll be home and applying to NYU.

A couple of Hells Angels bikers, bandannas over their scraggly ponytails, smoke pot in front of a lumpy stone sculpture outside the massive gray tower. She hears long, noisy tokes as she pulls open the door. She steps inside quickly to get away from their leering.

She feels like she's made an entrance in a play, or maybe a circus. Vibrations of fluorescent pink, orange and purple throb from every wall. Even the ceiling is buzzing color. The colors push up a memory from years ago when her mother went back to school to become a painter. Before the bad times. She told Billie that colors were made of waves that bounce against each other.

The image surfaces now, which makes her think of her mother, which makes her feel guilty, then angry.

It's her life, and she's living it in Technicolor.

"And is there care in heaven? And is there love in heavenly spirits to these creatures base?"

A shirtless man wearing a fringed leather vest is performing to an audience of one — a woman in a flowing dress who is gazing up at him adoringly.

"*The Faerie Queene*," the woman purrs, "blows my mind."

Dissonant notes of music. Billie's eyes swivel to pick out a girl sitting on a couch with a guitar. A huge man with a spiky Afro is curled around her, his fingers wrapping her hand, helping her to form chords. She frowns in concentration and strums awkwardly.

"Four strong winds that blow ..."

A flat thump vibrates as she stops to change the chord.

"... lonely. Seven seas that run ..."

A small boy not much older than little Joey is standing in front of them, sucking his thumb, watching. His wide eyes are barely visible through his mane of soft brown curls.

"... high."

She scans the room for Martin. In the middle of the room a blackboard on wheels divides the space. A man with frizzed black hair bounces in front of it, a piece of chalk and a spoon in one hand, a plastic tub of yogurt in the other. A knot of people pool on the floor by his feet. He alternates writing equations on the board with spooning yogurt into his mouth.

"Einstein predicted the existence of black holes — the equation is basic." Scribble, scribble. Scoop, swallow. "But now we've seen them. We know they really exist. Black holes change everything!"

From the edge of the room, the *pock-pock* sound of a ping-pong game holds down the stumbling rhythm to "Four Strong Winds," *The Faerie Queene* and Einstein.

Pock-pock …

"Massive objects cause distortion in space-time …"

Pock-pock …

"You came."

He pierces the vision. Hugs her. Quickly. Like an old friend. Like she's supposed to be there.

"Of course."

She takes in his momentary appraisal, his warm smile.

"Let's see what making history looks like." He slips his arm through hers and guides her to the elevator with smooth steps timed to "Four Strong Winds." At the seventh floor, the door opens to a purple lobby of activity and a beat decidedly rock and roll, not folk.

"This way." Martin pulls her to the right and they run an obstacle course of bodies — vertical and horizontal — smoking, drinking, necking. They turn right again into a corridor of open doors, gateways to a cauldron of music and voices. Martin stops in front of the only closed door. He pulls out a set of keys.

"Welcome to the Ashram Lounge."

She is confronted by a wall of smoke, a stew of mustardy-smelling tobacco blended with the sweet softness of pot. A familiar blend from her childhood. The fog diffuses the light and shadow from the television. Her eyes adjust and she interprets couches and chairs under piles of bodies. The floor is alive, a mass of people moving in slow motion as though they are part of some elaborate dance. Candles glow, and pinpricks of light from cigarettes and joints dapple the room.

She crossed rooms like this when she was little. Barefoot in a nightie, navigating by the flickering light of the television, tiptoeing past sleeping grown-ups from bedroom to kitchen to get a drink of milk.

She shakes off little girl Missy's past and steps into Billie's present. Now it's her turn to be an adult.

The serious reporting voices of Huntley and Brinkley recite percentages of returns in eastern polling stations. She lets her body melt into the room and onto the floor, just like the candle castle on the table, where pooling rivulets recongeal, unrecognizable. Martin hands her a beer and her fingers curl around the stubby bottle, imprinting into the beads of condensation. She blows softly across the neck and produces a low tugboat echo.

The soundtrack of her childhood has the gentle clink of ice cubes, but she can fill her own soundtrack with tugboats if she wants.

"NBC is projecting that Governor Wallace has won the state of Louisiana with 55 percent of the vote."

"Wallace?!" A voice from the couch.

"None of it matters, they're all the same." A voice from the floor. "Humphrey's just Johnson's pet. Nixon's a creep. Put racist Wallace into the mix and the country's fucked."

Martin takes a deep toke on a joint and passes it to her. She lets the smell curl around her hand, caress her hair. She's smoked a bit with Dan, but the smell always brings back memories of her father.

To hell with it, she thinks. *I am Billie Taylor, exile, and I can do whatever the hell I want.*

She takes a deep toke, exhales and passes the joint back to Martin.

"Nixon continues to maintain his lead in the state of New Hampshire."

Martin is a dragon, smoke pouring from his nostrils, his eyes blazing red.

"Change isn't going to happen in the election box." He inhales and speaks through his held breath. "The revolution is on the street. Either you're in, or you're out."

She takes the joint and breathes the smoke in, holding it in her lungs as she watches a large dog wearing a red bandanna nose its way through the room inhaling bits of leftover pizza. She worries he might choke on the popcorn that dusts the floor like snow. But the dog happily vacuums across the common room before flopping down beside Billie, wedging her into Martin.

"In Maine, 69 percent of the vote is in and NBC has projected that Hubert Humphrey will carry the state of Maine."

"One summer, I stayed with my cousin at a cottage in Maine." Martin's voice is close, intimate. "We built a tree fort."

Billie hands him back the joint. His words have become over-articulated, rehearsed. "His father was a four-star general. World War Two. Korea. They went from base to base, but we always got together at Thanksgiving." Martin's head is a pointy boulder on her shoulder. "My cousin signed up right away. He was going to show his dad. He was going to get more medals." He holds the smoke in his lungs. "Got lots of medals the day he was blown up by a land mine," he says as he exhales.

"... 62 percent of the vote is now in from Illinois ... for all intents and purposes they both have 46 percent of the vote."

"His father saluted the coffin as it went down. His mother held the folded flag in her lap. Dry-eyed, both of them."

The dog rolls over and farts. She hopes Martin doesn't think it's her. It's like a decayed fish.

"You would have taken a great picture of that funeral. You've got an eye." He holds the joint out to her, but she waves it away. The pain of loss is getting too strong.

"Photographs change people's minds. They show the truth. They can make a difference." He's delicately playing with the ends of her hair. "That picture by Schutzer, of the Marine walking with the two young kids, one of them with his head melting from napalm. That convinced me we were on the wrong side of this thing."

"Vermont, by NBC projection, has gone for Nixon."

"He used a Leica for that shot." Martin rests his warm palm on her neck. "He died two years later, on assignment."

Billie has read about Schutzer. His photo of a captured Viet Cong soldier had been the cover of *Life* in November, 1965. His death last year while on assignment in Israel rocked the world of journalism.

She blows a tugboat sound and swallows a mouthful of beer.

"For me it was Catherine Leroy. Her photo of a woman lying on the ground with her dead baby, on the road to Hué."

She hasn't talked to anyone, not really talked, since she left the city. It feels good.

"The presidential election is going to hinge on the results from California and the vote from California is coming into our Election Central slowly."

Martin's voice is hard-edged. "We need to wake the Canadians up to what's going on. No one is innocent."

Joints are passed, cigarettes glow in overfull ashtrays, eventually the beer is lukewarm. A quarter past twelve, and there is still no clear winner of the presidential race. The room feels like three-day-old soup that's been reheated too often.

Martin softly caresses her ankle. "You're a good photographer, you know."

"I know," she says with a small laugh.

"Bring me anything you think will work for the newsletter. We need your eye. You can make a difference." His hand travels under her bell-bottoms to her calf. But she's not ready for anything more.

"I've got to head back."

He nods and she extricates herself from the dog, the vomit-green carpet and slow buzz of the room that is far too comfortable. She takes the elevator down with a freak who is tripping.

"Humphrey Dumphrey. Nixon Dickson. Doesn't matter," he croons as his hands dance. "Doesn't matter, doesn't matter, doesn't matter. Remember what the Dormouse said. Bang. The kids are dead tomorrow. We're all dead tomorrow."

You're a good photographer ... You can make a difference.

TWENTY-THREE

Dear Dan,

I met a guy who puts out a newsletter called The American Exile in Canada. They're using a photo I took at a protest. I told him about you and RITA and he said to be careful. He said that training changes a person.

Is that why you haven't written?

She tears up the letter and burns the pieces in the ash-tray. *P.S. Don't write. The Feds read the mail.*

She realizes that there is no way to get the prints to Jack. She'll have to take them with her. When she leaves.

By the next morning, the vote is too close to call. No one knows who the next President of the United States will be.

It's thirty-six hours before Hubert Humphrey calls Richard Milhous Nixon in tears to concede. The 37th President of the United States vows to bring the country together and to end the war. Everyone wants to believe him.

Change isn't going to happen in the ballot box. The revolution is in the street.

Bitter November damp seeps up from the grimy concrete on her walk from the gray school to the gray subway. Cheryl has cut back Billie's hours at the Mynah Bird. "No one is coming for the music anymore. Just for the strippers." Her bikini uniform has been traded for a tight white sweater. The tips are smaller. She'll be lucky to make twenty bucks this weekend.

She turns up Bedford Road and the heavy grease smell from Harvey's follows her, reminding her of how hungry she is. Is it her turn to make dinner tonight? Did her mother tell her to pick something up at the store? The body bags pile up and all they talk about is meal planning!

But when she turns the key in the door, she's coated by the seductive tang of Maurice's Meatloaf, a dish named after an old flame of her mother's. The smell turns up the dial and her brain jolts as though she's had a hit of caffeine. Her taste buds anticipate the unexpected blend of hamburger, tomato soup, mustard and green pepper. Delicious on mashed potatoes.

She won't let herself be comforted. She slaps down the thought of pleasure and slams the front door on the gray frozen world.

There's laughter in the kitchen. Billie can't remember the last time her mother laughed.

She walks down the hall and stops at the kitchen door. Across from her mother, a young man turns his head and then quickly stands to greet her, unbalancing her anger.

"Oh, hello. You must be Billie. Your mother's been telling me all about you."

He holds out a smooth hand, his bright pink palm looking vulnerable against his dark skin. His hair close-cropped waves, his body straight and proud.

"Henry."

Her hand floats up to meet his.

"Yikes, your hand is cold! You need a cup of this great hot chocolate your mom made for me."

He lifts a mug from the rack, takes a ladle from beside the stove and spoons hot chocolate from a pot. He hands it to her with grace and she wraps her rigid fingers around it.

"Thanks," she mumbles. "How can anyone live in this freezing, godforsaken country?" She sips the hot chocolate.

"Well, right now this country is looking like a bit of heaven to me." Henry's voice is warm, the vowels soft and round.

Of course. A dodger.

Her mother gets up and starts to set the table.

"Here, let me do that, Jean."

Her mother smiles as she hands him the cutlery and goes to mash the potatoes. Billie stands in the doorway, watching them as though they are in a play. "Where did you cross?"

"Buffalo. A few hours ago. Went right to TADP. Mark directed me here. I tell you the whole thing is like a fairy tale. I left the ogre's house and have come to a magical kingdom where everyone is nice, and good, and kind."

Billie bristles. "Welcome to exile in a very cold magical kingdom. Siberia."

"Well, yes, it is a bit brisk," he laughs. He clearly is not rising to her bait. "But not that different from Philly." She watches as he carefully straightens the knives and forks to line up with the plaid pattern of the tablecloth.

"That's where you're from? Philadelphia?"

Henry nods. "My father drove me to Buffalo this morning. And then across the border. Told them we were just visiting for the day. No luggage, so they believed him. Then he left me at the bus station in Niagara Falls, on the Canadian side. Bought me the ticket to Toronto."

"He did that for you?" She thought of Kenny and Linda with families ready to disown them.

"He's a lawyer. I'm his only son. We're close. He didn't want to see me come home in a box."

"Couldn't you have gone to college and got a deferment?"

"I am in college. Or rather I *was* in college. My first year. Studying to be a social worker." He folds the napkins carefully.

"So why didn't you get a deferment?"

"Deferments are off now. The draft boards have the final say on who gets called up. And it seems those draft boards like killing off Black boys even more than killing off White boys."

Her mother scoops the potatoes into a bowl. "U of T has a good social work program. Once you get settled, you can apply, probably start up next fall —"

"Next fall? I have to wait a whole year?"

Billie recognizes the sound of lost dreams.

Her mother touches his shoulder lightly. "You're only nineteen. A year is no time. It will fly by. And until then you can do lots of volunteer work to show the school how committed you are. They might offer you a scholarship. But one step at a time. Right now, it's time to eat."

Henry accepts a plate from her mother. Meatloaf, green peppers and mashed potatoes are covered in a sauce that Billie thinks of as the essence of home. Despite herself, she savors every mouthful.

"This is amazing, Jean."

Billie's jaw clenches at the happiness she sees in her mother's face. The meal feels like a family dinner.

Family. She will not be enticed by the smells and the smiles, the laughter and the love, by the —

"Billie, don't you need to get to work?"

Instantly, the world is filled with sharp edges again.

Henry gets up from the table as she stands. "Let me walk you there," he says, heading toward the hall.

"No. I mean, I'm fine, thanks. It's just a couple of blocks." And she swoops up her coat and is out the door, feeding her anger.

When our actions do not, our fears do make us traitors.

She will not be a traitor. She will act. Somehow.

TWENTY-FOUR

After a weekend of offensive drunks at the Mynah Bird and no word from Martin, she needs to talk to someone real. Someone who is not her mother.

So even though it's Sunday and she's only had five hours of sleep, she's up early making bran muffins, hoping to see Henry.

The percolator pops the bitter, nutty smell of coffee with each bubble that bursts against the lid. She thinks a perking coffee pot is probably the most optimistic sound in the world. The promise that today will be better.

She wants this to be the first sound Henry hears. She

wants the smell to wake him.

But there is only silence from his room, and it's her mother who arrives in the kitchen first.

She pours her mother a coffee. She counted her savings last night when she got home. Three hunderd dollars. More than halfway there. She knows it will be hard for her mother at the start, but she'll get used to it. They can both start new lives.

"Thank you." Her mother's gratitude irritates her. "Muffins?"

"I thought Henry might like some," she says, oven mitt in hand, reaching for the tray.

As she says it, there's a blast of cold behind her. The back door opens and Henry steps in, swirling with fresh, fall damp air. She's frozen like a stage tableau, surprised by the fact of him there, when she'd been picturing his head on a pillow. Surprised to see him closing the door on a rare morning of November beauty, a morning of startling black branches against a cobalt sky.

"I could smell that coffee all the way down the lane! And muffins! A perfect first course."

He sets a paper bag onto the picnic table and sits on the bench, carefully untying the laces on his polished brown leather shoes — good quality, like the tailored camel-hair coat he hangs on the rack beside the door.

"I thought I might make us a big Sunday brunch. It's the least I can do for your hospitality. I make a mean omelet! Mushrooms, peppers, cheese, okay? And I saw something in that corner store, Becker's, something called peameal bacon. Apparently, Canadians have their own kind of bacon! So I had to get some to try it, to help me become more Canadian."

Henry gently takes over the kitchen, taking control of the tenuous armistice between Billie and her mother. She sets the muffins out to cool.

"Mark gave me some rooms to check out yesterday. There's lots of places for rent. But the way I see it, there's no point in knocking on people's doors first thing on Sunday morning. Some of those folks might be churchgoers and all. So I'll get a move on that this afternoon."

Billie wonders how Henry can be so close to her age — younger than Dan — and yet seem of a whole other generation. He's the most cheerful draft dodger she's met. She watches as he pours a coffee, heats up the griddle and fills the kitchen with the smell of "Canadian" bacon. He chops the vegetables precisely. He breaks eggs into a bowl with one hand and whisks with the other.

"Mark said that there isn't any particular part of town for Black folks. He says most people won't have a problem with my skin."

"I think he's right. I think it's different here." Her mother's morning voice is soft.

The smell of the peppers, mushrooms, eggs and cheese match the sunshine of the day.

"Did you know that the escaping slaves called Canada heaven in their spirituals? It was a code for the Promised Land. I think I've arrived!"

Irritation begins to creep under Billie's skin. She wonders about Gina and Lester. Would this seem like the "Promised Land" to the Black Panthers?

She watches Henry making breakfast and thinks of Lester making breakfasts for the hungry kids in Harlem.

How can he ignore what's happening back home? How can he just walk away?

"Did you do any work with the Panthers?" His head jerks and then refocuses on the omelet.

"The Panthers are well meaning," he says, plunging bread into the toaster, "but I don't think inciting violence will help their cause."

She ignores the warning bells and quotes Gina. "Revolutions never come about peacefully."

"Billie." Her mother's voice is sharp. "Not everyone is looking for a revolution."

She can't let it go. *We revolt simply because, for many reasons, we can no longer breathe* … Was that what it said on that poster at the UAE? Was it Frantz Fanon? "You should go to the Union of American Exile office. Meet Martin. Being a political exile is about more than dodging Vietnam."

Henry hands her a plate filled with omelet, toast and bacon but doesn't meet her eyes.

"Right now, I'm not looking to be an American exile. I'm going to work on becoming a landed immigrant and I hope, one day, a Canadian citizen. I can't go back home, maybe not ever, so I need to go forward. I need to make this country my new home."

"But you can't close your eyes to what is going on!"

"My eyes are open. It's just that they are looking in a different direction."

"That's not enough. Have you read *The Wretched of the Earth* by Frantz Fanon? It's about …" What was it Jack had said? "… it's about how you can't be free until you've thrown off the yoke of colonialism."

All warmth has gone out of Henry's face. "I don't need anyone to coach me in the history of slavery," he says quietly.

Her mother lays her hand on Henry's. "Billie's boyfriend is in the forces. She's finding the move to Canada difficult."

"Don't make excuses for me! You don't know anything about my life."

So much for the truce.

They chew in silence.

"This is delicious, Henry. Thank you," her mother offers, trying to get them back on track.

"Glad you like it." Henry replies, but his smile's wattage has dimmed.

"More coffee?"

"Thank you, no." Henry stands and takes his empty plate to the sink. "I think I'll just have a little walk around, enjoy the quiet sunshine of a November Sunday." He reaches for his coat and slips on his shoes. "I'll head back to the TADP office and take a look at the job board, then check out those rooms for rent."

Her mother goes to him. "We'll be here." She puts her hands on his arms. "There'll be chili in the pot, ready for whenever you're back."

Henry nods and is gone. Billie stares at the brown smear of Heinz 57 sauce left on her plate. Then she's up, her mind cold steel as she leaves the plate, the kitchen and the house, slamming the front door on her uneaten bran muffins, pulling her coat around her as she stamps down to College Street to find refuge in the public library, where she retrieves a copy of *The Wretched of the Earth*.

... the European peoples must first decide to wake up and shake themselves, use their brains and stop playing this stupid game of Sleeping Beauty.

She reads until the library closes, only understanding half of what she reads. She checks out the book and clutches it as she walks in circles around Queen's Park, avoiding the simmering pot of chili, returning only when she knows they will both be asleep.

At school, she props *The Wretched of the Earth* defiantly on her desk, waiting to be challenged. It connects her to the world outside of sleepy Toronto. It's Veterans Day — Remembrance Day, the Canadians call it — and when they stand at 11:00 to remember the war dead, she holds *The Wretched of the Earth* against her heart.

At the level of individuals, violence is a cleansing force.

Talk doesn't change anything. Talk is not action. Henry becoming a good little Canadian won't do anything to stop the war and the murder of children.

No. The only question, ever, is which action to take.

To make a choice.

Revolutions never come about peacefully.

Desperate times call for desperate measures.

TWENTY-FIVE

It was dark on her way to school, and it is dark on her way home. She decides to walk to save the fare, but also to have time alone. Veterans Day has made her thoughtful. *Violence is a cleansing force.* Billie again comes home into laughter and the unmistakable smell of cooking.

"Tonight's a celebration," her mother calls from across the room.

Henry beams. "Yup. Day three in Toronto with two job offers and one clean room in a house with no cockroaches."

"You're leaving?" She says it before she can censor out the hurt.

"That's the rule, Billie," her mother says quickly. "It's what we agree to with TADP. Three days for each dodger. Just until they get settled."

Henry spoons stew into individual bowls. She watches rivers of stew slide over chunks of potato.

"Listen, I just have to say how amazing it's been to be here. What you two are doing is phenomenal. You don't know what it's like to have to leave everybody you love, without knowing if you'll ever go back. It broke my heart to say goodbye to my grandmother. She's not doing well, and I may never see her again. When my father left me at that bus station, it was the loneliest moment of my life. But then I thought of what it would be like for them if I came home in a box."

She presses and splits open a potato. Dark gravy seeps between the tines of her fork.

"So, I've made you a specialty from my house — Mrs. O'Malley's Irish stew. Thickened with a hunk of bread slathered in mustard. It's the only way I know how to say thank-you to you two. I don't know what the future will be but you both have given me a good start. Bon appetit. Oh, and there's cherry cheesecake for dessert, because I hear it's your favorite." Her eyes are fixed on her fork.

It takes strength not to hurl the dishes, launch potato and meat stew grenades, cleanse this scene with the splatter of cheesecake onto the walls, watch it all melt and drip onto the floor.

She will not get sucked into their blind little world. She will not shut her eyes. She will be brave. Violence is a cleansing force.

❧

Every night that week, the news is filled with new horrors.

Twig bodies are piled up in mass graves.

Bulldozers clear forests.

Napalm incinerates villages.

Children run screaming from burning houses.

Mothers wail by the side of dirt roads, clutching dead babies.

Walter Cronkite travels with bombers on a mission and even he is shocked.

Bombs are dropped into lush jungles and there are too many to bury as flies crawl across the eyes of bloated dead bodies.

The world is a tornado twisting into a chaos of hell. And all people do is talk.

On Saturday, she splurges on two Danish pastries and two coffees and heads to the UAE office.

The room is alive with the clacking of his typewriter. She walks in to the *clang-smack* as he sends the carriage over to begin the new line.

Martin's writer's scowl transforms into a smile when he sees her.

"Coffee?"

"And Danish." She smiles back.

"With coffee and Danish, we can change the world."

"Does it ever make you angry?" She plops herself into the dusty armchair and squeaks the lid off her Styrofoam cup.

"What? Coffee and Danish?"

She snorts through the steam of her coffee. "No. Being forced to live here. Nobody does anything here. They just talk. Talk, talk, talk all the time. They just don't get it. How can you stand it?"

He puts his coffee down. Takes her seriously. She feels the shift.

"It was hard in the beginning, sure. I felt like I'd run smack into a brick wall of marshmallows."

She laughs.

When he speaks again, his voice is unguarded. "But I thought it was probably better than jail. Still do."

"But weren't you in college? Couldn't you have gotten deferment and avoided getting drafted?"

"Deferment is a lie. They'll take you if they want you. Especially if they want to punish you. And the Feds wanted to punish me."

She waits. He blows on his coffee.

"I was in Ann Arbor. University of Michigan. I'd started getting political, joined the SDS. So I was already into it when the university handed over student records to the Feds."

"The university handed over your records? Why?"

"Because the Feds wanted them. They had a ranking system. If your marks were low, you'd get drafted and sent over."

"What? You mean they could target you if you didn't do well at school?"

"Yup. Your marks slip and the punishment is getting your head blown off on the other side of the world."

"The administration fed into the draft board? That's outrageous! Couldn't you stop them?"

"Oh, we tried. There were sit-ins. There was a referendum. But they weren't interested in the referendum and they banned the sit-ins. So there I was, eighteen, eligible for the draft, whether I was in school or not, and told I couldn't protest. So much for democracy."

"So you came to Canada?"

She watches him chew. A flake of icing is on the corner of his lip.

"No. Not then. I cleared out of Ann Arbor and went home to Grand Haven. Thought I'd just hang out on the beach for a bit. Try to get my head together. But it turned out I was on the Selective Service hit list. They were waiting for me. I'd been busted for possession a few months back and they said they'd clear the charge if I signed up. Just like that. They said if I didn't enlist, they'd make sure the charge stuck. Not much of a choice. Go to jail for possession and rot there for twenty years, or take the roll of the dice."

His eyes flick to hers. She watches him lick his sticky fingers.

"You signed up."

He nods.

She thinks of Dan. "What was it like?"

"Boot camp was worse than any hell you can imagine."

The room is still.

"We were doing a simulation. I'm squatting in a hole, tall grass all around, and I'm looking for target cutouts of little brown people to shoot. Five officers are sitting under a tree, smoking. They've bullied and tortured me for the past six months. They're laughing in the shade, and I'm sweating in a hole and I think, *How many of them could I shoot before they shoot me?* I looked at each one of them in my sights. *Could I get two? Maybe three?* I've been well trained. *If I could get three, is it worth it?*"

The question fills the room.

"My finger is on the trigger. It's a simple calculation. If I can guarantee shooting three of them before they kill me, I'll do it. But I didn't think two was worth it. I thought my life was worth more than just two of theirs."

He raises his eyes. She's frozen, caught in his sights.

"Two wasn't enough."

He crumples the paper from the Danish. Does a perfect rim toss into the trash can.

"I had a three-day leave. I headed home. Everyone was all proud of me with my buzzed hair and my uniform. I asked my uncle if I could borrow my dead cousin's car, told him I wanted to go upstate to visit my girl. And then I drove to Detroit. Didn't stop. Just drove on coffee and cigarettes. I used my dead cousin's ID when I crossed — it was still in the glove compartment — and said I was visiting a friend in Waterloo. That part was true. I had the name and address of a professor. A guy who'd come to the sit-in in Michigan. I had nothing with me, no bags or anything. It looked like I was coming for a day trip, so they waved me through. When I got to Waterloo, I spent three days shaking. Shaking and vomiting. I was sure that the Feds were going to grab me and haul my ass back to the States, throw me in a cell for the rest of my life. But Professor McFadden said they weren't allowed to do that. He said Prime Minister Trudeau had made that clear. Dodging the draft or deserting from the army has nothing to do with Canadian law. I had broken no laws. I just had to figure out how to live my life here."

He offers her a cigarette. Their faces are close when she stretches to light hers from his lighter. She leans back into her chair to exhale. He clicks the Zippo closed.

"It took me a while to get up the nerve to call my folks. My father said I'd betrayed the family and betrayed the country. He said he was ashamed of me and he didn't ever want to see me again. My mother just cried."

She watches him exhale. "How did you end up in Toronto?"

"McFadden told me about Rochdale. Said the best thing I could do was go back to school and that Rochdale was free. I just had to make some bread to cover rent. So I came. There was no building then, classes were held in any spaces we could find. When the building went up, I finally felt safe. There are about a hundred of us dodgers and deserters living there now. There's no way the Feds can get in." His face opens to a wide smile. "Hell, even the cops have to rely on the protection of our security guys. Toronto's finest pigs are guarded by Hells Angels! I think that may be the definition of a free society."

"So you go through all of that and then — what? Edit a paper for exiles and let it all play out back home?"

He gets up and crosses around the desk to stand behind her. She feels his long fingers drumming on the back of the chair. "Hardly. Here I can fight without watching over my shoulder all the time. Here I can organize and not rot in a jail cell." His voice is like a jaguar on the prowl. "Here I can make the bastards pay."

She feels his hand graze her hair and rest on her neck. Out the window she sees tiny flakes of snow spiraling in the gray light. She lets the warmth of his hand spread across her shoulders.

"Look, a couple of us are going to spend Thanksgiving weekend at a farm in the country. People I think you should meet. Can you get the weekend off? Pick you up Saturday morning?"

People I think you should meet …

Her mother is predictably furious.

"Thanksgiving?"

"Well, American Thanksgiving. You and I have already had *Canadian* Thanksgiving."

Billie talks quickly to try to get out with as little damage as possible. "A few people from University of Waterloo — there's a big group of dodgers there. One of the profs has a farm he lets people use for retreats. Perfectly safe. University friends."

"But what about work?"

"I'm taking a night off. Tips are so bad it hardly makes a difference." She makes the plan nonnegotiable.

"But it's Thanksgiving. I've invited Doris … Henry …"

The twisting hurt in her mother's voice sends Billie into the ring, fists up.

"What the hell does Doris have to do with anything? She hasn't given a damn about me *ever* and it is a bit late to start playing at being a grandmother now. Don't pretend we're a family!" She can't stop now that she's started. "And I don't have anything to be *thankful* for except, maybe, my camera and the fact that I have some darkroom privileges at the local jail. Which I got on my own with no help from you or anyone else."

She can't control what is spewing out of her mouth. Months of anger become an incinerating blast.

"So yes, on *American* Thanksgiving, I am going to get out of here for one night and be with some friends who give a damn about me!"

She blazes out of the kitchen, refusing to feel for the woman she has left behind.

TWENTY-SIX

Billie's never spent time in the country. Scott is ecstatic to lend her his sleeping bag — apparently every Canadian boy has a sleeping bag. The inside blue plaid is permeated with a heavy, musty smell. Woodsmoke and boy sweat. She makes some brownies, packs the sleeping bag, a towel, a pillow and six bottles of a beer called Black Label.

She feels adventurous and vaguely pioneer. She brings her camera, like any tourist.

She hasn't spoken to her mother since yesterday morning. She refuses to feel guilty. Let her mother have dinner with bloody Doris and Goody Two-shoes Henry if that's what she wants. Let them have a pretend family dinner.

Martin arrives in his "valiant Valiant." It's an odd shade of green, and it ticks and rattles as she pulls open the heavy door.

"The heat's on the fritz, so you'll have to sit close. Spread the warmth."

Billie's old jacket is not up to the vague heating of the Valiant. Before they are even out of the city she's shivering.

"Isn't there any way to get heat out of that blower?"

By way of an answer, he pushes in the cigarette lighter. When it pops, he hands it to her. "That's as good as it gets. You cut your teeth on your first winter in Canada."

There will not be a second, she thinks. She may leave here with cut teeth — whatever that means — but she'll leave.

"You have to learn to be prepared. Like a Boy Scout." He stretches his right arm into the back seat to rifle in his duffle bag, while his left hand keeps a vague contact with the steering wheel. "Here. I brought you a present."

He hands her a rainbow-colored knit cap — "Canadians call it a toque" — and a pair of huge black-and-white mittens shaped like cow faces. She bursts out laughing.

"Who says Canadians aren't any fun?"

She pulls the cap over her hair, the mitts onto her hands and strikes a fashion pose.

"Yee-haw! Old MacDonald had a farm," he sings. "EE-I-EE-I-O."

The Naugahyde seat squeaks as Martin bounces and twitches. The concrete city drops away. Fewer and fewer cars. They turn off the main highway and cross over an invisible border. It's like arriving on a new square of a board game. They roll the dice and leave the square called Toronto, landing on the square called Ontario, Canada.

The square is made of flat fields and long straight side roads. A grid system that was parceled out to colonial settlers in the nineteenth century. Dutch and German names on mailboxes. Plowed fields of rock-hard furrows show a slip of frosted decoration. The sky is a threatening slate gray.

Billie points to slat fences snaking across fields.

"Snow fences," he says, "to direct snow drifts. Apparently you can't make it fall somewhere else. Like Florida."

The roads get thinner. They pass a black horse-drawn buggy with a bright-orange yield sign on the back. The horse's pace is a brisk clip-clop-clip-clop.

"Mennonites. Like our Amish." Martin roars past and sings louder. "With a neigh-neigh here and a neigh-neigh there."

Paved road becomes gravel, and they are bumping and swaying. Fat snowflakes are starting to stick to the windshield when they pull up to an isolated red brick farmhouse, the only building for miles.

There's another car in the gravel drive. A boxy Fiat station wagon with Quebec license plates and a faded bumper sticker. *Kennedy in '68*.

Smoke furls from the chimney down onto the roof before dissipating over the field. Steam is rising from half a dozen furry black cows standing silently in a field. Behind them, desiccated cornstalks rattle in the wind.

Billie swings her camera out as she opens the car door. The cattle stare silently as she takes time to focus.

"*All the cattle are standing like statues,*" sings Martin.

She's in the middle of a musical. *Oklahoma* in Southern Ontario. Where the corn was never as high as an elephant's eye.

Click. Wind.

She feels happy and free.

She feels like Billie Taylor.

He opens the back door to the farmhouse and she picks her way through a riot of boots and coats that block the entrance to the kitchen. A large woodstove commands the room and Billie is relieved by the toasty warm. There's a delicious smell of spaghetti sauce. A beanpole of a girl with a joint in one hand and a wooden spoon in the other stirs a pot. She flips her long braid behind her back as she turns to greet Billie.

"Hey. You must be Billie. I'm Vivien." She gestures vaguely at the stove. "The stove's called an Ashley," she says. "It's Ashley and I'm Vivien. Just like *Gone with the Wind.* Ashley Wilkes and Vivien Leigh. Get it?"

Martin bounds over like a retriever, dropping bags and groceries to pant in front of Vivien.

"Martin's more Mr. Kennedy than Rhett Butler. Good boy," she says, blowing the smoke into his ear.

"Woof! Blow in my ear and I'll follow you anywhere." He grins stupidly.

A bearded face steps between Billie and her line of focus.

"Hello, Billie."

Deep-set eyes lock onto hers. She's thrown off-kilter as two worlds collide.

"Jack?"

"None other." He grins.

A heartbeat plays out the last scene they were in together. The apartment on 114th. Dan. Her eyes dart around the room until they land back on his face.

"He's not here."

She flushes with the effort of pushing Dan from her mind. But Jack spins and attacks Martin in a huge bear hug.

"Thanks for bringing her, man. It's good to see a familiar face."

"It seemed like a place she might want to be." There's an odd, coded sound to their conversation, as though there has been a lot of discussion about this beforehand.

The scene with Tracy, Jack and Dan shoots through her mind and she glances at Vivien. But Vivien's jaw is set in a no-nonsense frame. Vivien isn't someone Billie would want to meet in a dark alley.

Billie turns back to Jack warily.

"What are you doing here?"

"Having a pleasant retreat in the countryside," he answers with a smirk.

"No, I mean *here*, in Canada." She knows that Jack would never willingly choose to come to Canada. "You get drafted? Deserting or dodging? Why didn't you answer my letters? I'm trying to get back to New York and I need a place to stay."

If Jack is here, that means one less couch to sleep on.

"There was some trouble in Chicago." His finger proudly traces a jagged half-circle scar above his right eyebrow.

Some trouble in Chicago. Images from the news play like the driving riff of a snare drum. Cars on fire. Rocks hurled through the air. Shattered glass windows. Bodies on the streets.

"I needed to disappear. I connected with folks in Montreal who helped get the Feds off my trail. Turns out you can do a lot more when you're invisible."

"Here?" The surprise of Jack crashing into her weekend

makes her belligerent. "How does hanging out in a farmhouse in the middle of nowheresville Canada have anything to do with stopping the war in Vietnam?"

"That, my dear Billie, is exactly what we've come together to talk about."

And there it is.

The silence is punctuated by pops from the Ashley woodstove. In the silence, she is aware of being watched.

"The farmhouse gives us a bit of privacy. To make plans," Martin says. "The Feds don't come snooping around these Mennonite farms. They're scared of horses." He smiles at her.

It's a chess game. But she doesn't know the rules yet. She needs space to think.

She hands Jack the beers and brownies. "Okay if I check out the rest of the house?" She heads for the stairs.

"Be careful," Vivien calls after her. "No one's lived upstairs in two years."

Every step up to the second floor creaks noisily but gives her distance from the kitchen. Jack has brought the memory of Dan back with a force that's unbalanced her. But there's something else, too. She's been brought here for a reason.

There's a thick layer of dust and grime everywhere. Rough bare wood floors lead to four bedrooms. Only one houses a bed — a thin old iron bedstead supporting a bare stained mattress with springs and stuffing poking out. She guesses they won't be sleeping up here.

She's in the middle of nowhere. With three people she doesn't know very well. They are speaking in some kind of code. Snow is falling. Cattle are staring. The floors are a battlefield of dead flies. A rusty mousetrap holds a desiccated skeleton.

They want her here.

The team needs a good photographer.

When she comes down, she catches Vivien's eye. An ally or a conspirator?

"Where's the ...?"

"Bathroom's outside." Vivien's focus is on the spaghetti sauce. She gestures absently at the door. "To the right. Don't forget to dump in some ashes when you're finished."

Billie looks out the window. A small pile of snowflakes has mounded up on the sill.

"The bathroom's outside?"

"Or you can just pee on the snow, like we do." Martin laughs, but his attention is fully occupied dividing up a stash with Jack.

Pioneer spirit, Billie thinks. She puts on her boots, her coat, her toque and her cow mittens. She leaves the warmth of the kitchen and steps into Santa's wonderland. To the right of the house is a small building with a crescent-moon shape cut out of the door. The door latch is a wooden peg that she slides over. The door swings outward.

She's never used an outhouse before. She steps in and closes the door. Cold, dark claustrophobia closes in. In the twilight, she sees and raises a scarred toilet seat. She pops open her jeans and quickly sits down, only to pop up again with the shock of the cold on her bottom. She takes a deep breath and sits back down. Cold air blows up from the depths of god knows where.

Really? This is the best place they could meet? Her bladder tenses, freezing her desire to pee. But she forces herself to breathe slowly and relax, until hot urine splashes away from her, falling down into some unknown depth.

Jack. It's as though by reading *The Wretched of the Earth*

she's conjured him up. There's a steeliness about him that is new, like the scar above his eye. An edge that is surprisingly sexy, a thought she shoves away the moment it becomes visible.

Oatmeal-breath Jack, with the Feds on his trail.

When she automatically turns to flush, she remembers Vivien's last comment and sees a metal bucket on the floor beside her with a child's yellow plastic shovel sticking out of a mound of gray ash. She takes a scoop and plops it down into the hole.

She hopes to be constipated for the next twenty-four hours.

Outside, the glow from inside the farmhouse is reaching out to the snowflakes. There's a perfect window shape suspended in the air hovering above the ground. It's the only light in the darkness. She is alone, outside the frame.

She opens the door to a room transformed. Candlelight coats the corners in shadow. Vivien is wiping some plates. "Just getting off a bit of mouse turd." Beer, brownies, grass and cigarette papers litter the floor. Martin is buttering a loaf of French bread. She smells garlic. He wraps it in tin foil and places it on top of the Ashley.

Billie's unrolled sleeping bag has been moved to the green couch.

She pulls off a beer cap with the confidence of a soldier. Joining the ranks. The side of her that faces the Ashley is blazing and flushed. Her other side is cold until Martin comes up behind her. His heat radiates into her back.

"Happy Thanksgiving!" He clinks his beer bottle against hers.

Jack lights a large candle held to a tree stump by a mound of solidified wax. The spreading pool of light warms their skin tones.

Vivien proudly flourishes a bowl of cooked spaghetti.

The floor is their table. They sit cross-legged, balancing plates of spaghetti and garlic bread, cigarettes, joints and beer.

It's a Thanksgiving dinner of a new kind, with a new family.

She is aware, always, of the dark just beyond the edge of their circle — the dark and the snow and the unsaid.

"So, you knew each other in New York?" Vivien is abrupt. She wonders what Vivien knows already. She nods, not sure how far to go.

"Jack and my boyfriend were roommates."

"We were at Columbia." Jack drops a crumb of their story.

"You were at Columbia?" Vivien asks, looking at Billie as though she has suddenly come into focus.

"No," she says, glancing at Jack. "My boyfriend was at Columbia."

"But she went to the strike." Jack says it proudly, as though he has something to do with it. "Got roughed up. Took some great photos."

"You didn't tell me that," Martin says with a note of what sounds like envy.

Jack is animated. "That's where it started. And then there was Chicago." He turns to her. "You should have come."

Vivien unwraps a small brown cube from a silver paper.

"I know." Billie says it plainly, a simple statement of fact.

I would have, if Dan hadn't enlisted, if my mother hadn't turned me into an exile, if my entire life hadn't been yanked away from me.

Vivien sets her cigarette in the ashtray and puts the cube of hash on the lit end.

"Chicago was amazing!" Jack's knee is bouncing frenetically. "The marches, the street theater, each unit playing its part. It was the turning point. They'll never hold a Democratic convention again!"

Vivien bows her head over the cigarette and noisily sucks up the smoke. She passes the ashtray along to Jack.

"You should have come," Jack repeats, his voice strangled as he sucks the smoke. "It sure as hell opened Tracy's mind! In the end, she couldn't take it. Went back to her pom-poms." He laughs cynically. "But you ..." His eyes tighten on her face.

Yes, she should have been there. In the action, with her father's camera.

She won't be left behind again.

"We showed the world." The smoke falls out of Jack's mouth like a fog of dry ice. "Up until then, people thought there was still a point to elections. But *elected officials* ..." He says the words like he is scraping off dog turd. "... can't — won't — do anything. We showed the whole world that there's no such thing as representative democracy anymore."

She twirls her fork against her spoon, slowly building up a knot of spaghetti strands. She turns the fork around and around as Jack's voice deepens.

"We *knew* what Mayor Daley was going to do. We rehearsed for it. There was this moment ... I was standing on a hill, looking down at two armies. Like in *Henry V*."

"*The hum of either army stilly sounds* ..." Martin quotes.

"Exactly!" Jack gestures to an imaginary field on his right. "One army, a disciplined force in blue helmets. Straight lines. Massive. Armed to the teeth. The other ..." He spreads out his left arm. "Dancing! Singing songs of peace. Our rebel army, armed only with love."

She can see it. She is on the hillside.

Focus. Click. Wind.

"But Daley had his troops ready. They waited until it was dark, then they stampeded through the park, lobbing tear gas into our rainbow tents, smashing people with clubs, kicking, punching, leaving people bleeding in the grass, or throwing them into the paddy wagons."

Columbia. Heavy feet pounding up the stairs. Bulging blue bellies. *Click.* Fingernails in her scalp.

"But *we* were ready for *them*! We smeared ourselves with Vaseline so they couldn't grab us!" He laughs. "We answered the swing of clubs with chants. 'The whole world is watching!'"

"The whole world is watching! The whole world is watching!" chants Vivien, her eyes fierce.

Billie puts herself in the picture of Chicago, filling in the blank space where she should have been.

Jack's voice is old, an ancient storyteller in a cave, around the fire. "And the world *was* watching. They watched as we danced our way into police lines and the police unleashed the full force of their imperialistic rage on us. The air thick with smoke and rage. Smoke and rage."

Smoke pours from Jack's nostrils, a fog settling on the cold crusts of garlic bread and smears of sauce. "Then we weren't singing anymore. Chants of peace didn't silence the guns. We put our bodies on the gears of the death machine. If they wanted a war, then bring it on. We brought the war home." His hand fingers the scar above his eye.

Pictures from the nightly news flash in Billie's brain. A little child draped over the top of a pile of bodies on a jungle road. Flies buzzing beneath the voice of a journalist.

"The choice is obvious. To do nothing is to be a murderer."

The smoke, the beer, the candles, Jack's voice — all swirl together like an incantation.

She understands that this is a cliff. She is standing with her toes dug into the earth at the edge of the world.

"No one is innocent." His voice is harsh. "Least of all Canadians. Canadians are not neutral bystanders. They are selling planes and armaments to the States to use on the innocent victims of Vietnam. They are training and equipping the Saigon police."

The candlelight exaggerates the shadows. Jack's lips have the curl of a German shepherd.

"They must be stopped. By any means possible."

Martin's voice is quiet in her ear. "Not to act is to be a murderer."

Bring the war home.

The fire pops. Vivien hands her the last crust of garlic bread. "Desperate measures for desperate times."

Billie's brain is struggling to wrestle meaning from this moment. A drumbeat on her heart. *By any means possible.* Jack's face bursts into focus with the flash of a lighter. She watches him smoke in the dark — calm now, determined, illuminated only by the glow of the lit tobacco.

She loses sense of time. How long has she been sitting here? How long has her head been resting on Martin's shoulder?

"You take the couch," he says gently, stretching out her sleeping bag. He unrolls his own on the floor. She navigates her way to the distant dark island and pulls the bag over her clothes. The musty boy-smell coats and soothes her. Her tired brain lets go of the room and falls into a dreamless sleep.

❧

There is a wonderful smell, a delicious smell, a dark, earthy, warm and happy smell.

Billie opens her eyes.

Coffee. The room is light gray. She turns her head and sees Martin standing by the woodstove. Warm currents are rolling over her head but have yet to reach her feet. She unfurls as Martin hands her a mug. She sits up and lets the warmth of the cup work its magic.

"Good morning." His smile is intimate.

Steam coats her face. Moisture condenses on her cold skin, and she's left with warm rivulets weaving along her cheeks. She sips the coffee. Martin stares out the window. The icy room is filled with soft warm breathing.

The morning has a normalcy to it, dictated by the joy of bacon and eggs cooked on the Ashley. Martin does breakfast duty and shows her how to balance slices of bread into a wire "toaster" and place it on the stovetop.

After breakfast, Martin and Jack go outside to split and stack wood to replace what they've used. Billie and Vivien wash dishes in water heated on the Ashley.

"Martin says you're planning to go back to New York." Vivien says it as an accusation.

"As soon as I can. As soon as I can make enough money and find a place to stay."

"But Jack told me all of your friends are gone. Your boyfriend's in the army." She hands her a plate to dry. "I can't understand why you'd go back."

"It's my home. I'm nothing but an exile here."

Vivien snorts. "We're all exiles. None of us have a home. They've stolen our home from us. We're at war."

"But if I stay here, I'll have to do another year of high school."

"Really? That's your problem? Children are being murdered every day, and you're worried about finishing high school? There's no one back there for you. And you'd have to spend all your time earning money just to get by. But here you've got rent covered, basic needs covered and you can make a difference." Vivien passes her another wet plate.

"Why did you come to Canada? Why didn't you stay in the States to fight?"

"I came up with a deserter. We'd been together for a year when he got drafted. When he came back on leave, he was a mess. Told me what was really happening in Vietnam. I knew I had to get him out. We crossed in Vermont and went to Montreal. That's where we met Jack."

"Where is he? The deserter?"

"Up north. Place called Killaloe. Ted's a casualty of the war. 'Nam fried him. He went back to the land to try to get his head together." Vivien's hands are still in the greasy water. "When he took off, I thought about going back. But Jack convinced me to stay and work with the movement in Montreal. I've been organizing marches. But that's not enough." She turns to Billie. "Look, it doesn't matter where you are. Once you see the lie for what it is, you can't run away from it. Not if you have any kind of heart beating in your chest."

Billie hears the harshness of the accusation.

"Karl Marx said, 'Things do not have to be the way they are.'" Vivien closes the cupboard door with a firm click.

"Sounds like this girl Tracy didn't have the courage to change things. But you? If you can save one life, don't you think it's worth it? You can change history." Vivien faces Billie head-on. "Or you can walk away."

It's dusk when Martin pulls the car up in front of her house. She reaches into the back to grab the sleeping bag and her pack.

"I'll be in touch."

She turns to face him.

I'll be in touch.

She slides across the squeaky Naugahyde and opens the door. As she steps out, he leans across the seat.

"There's a protest on Saturday. Down Yonge Street to city hall." His voice is clear, in charge. "Take your camera."

The Valiant pulls away, leaving her facing a dark house. She hopes her mother is out.

I'll be in touch.

Her thumb runs along the ridges of her key. She smiles as she slides it in.

She is part of a plan.

Take your camera …

TWENTY-SEVEN

Two lines of protesters, marching peacefully, two abreast on each sidewalk on an icy Saturday, slow the traffic along Dundas Street. She skirts around them, weaving through stopped cars, running ahead to try to get a shot. Searching for a glimpse of Martin.

Tailored suits and coats mingle with miniskirts atop frosty pink legs. Leather fringes, bell-bottoms and caftans poke from under sheepskin jackets and worn wool coats.

"Left, right, LBJ. How many kids did you kill today?" The chant repeated, setting the pace of the marchers. "Left, right, LBJ. How many kids did you kill today?"

Signs lift and fall into the rhythm:

We Refuse to Go!

Stop the Bombing!

Get Out of Vietnam NOW!

But there's another group on the other side of the street. All men. In tight, tidy suits and ties. Carrying an American flag.

Stop the Spread of Communism!

Better Dead than Red!

Counter-protesters. The marchers turn down Bay Street, and for a moment she has a glimpse of both sides, set against the backdrop of Chinatown, their placards surrounded by signs in Chinese and old bearded men standing in narrow doorways, watching. She focuses her camera as she walks.

The marchers spill out onto the large square of the new city hall, an odd mushroom of a building, where thousands of protesters have set up banners.

"Ho, Ho, Ho Chi Minh! Ho, Ho, Ho Chi Minh!"

"Go home, Commies!"

Her eyes dart. A flare could ignite and turn the day violent. But this is Toronto, not Chicago, and all she sees are peaceful protesters and peaceful counter-protesters. And journalists with microphones and cameras.

She sidles up to a man with a microphone interviewing two young men — one in a tidy suede jacket, the other in a suit.

"And you, sir, you are an American, of draft age, living in Canada. Tell me, are you a draft dodger?"

"Yes. Yes, I am."

"Why have you chosen to avoid the draft?"

"Because I am a pacifist and I don't believe in what the United States is doing now."

A pacifist? She wants to hit him. The time for pacifism is over.

"And you, sir. You are a Canadian?"

"Yes, I am."

"What do you think about this protest? What do you think about the American involvement in Vietnam?"

"Well, actually, I wish Canada was in it. I'd like to go. Get it done. Get it over with. Get rid of the Communist menace." The journalist says nothing, just nods his head.

Billie's rage hits the top of her skull. Why doesn't the journalist challenge this guy? She's screaming before she's had a chance to think.

"Jesus, how can you be so complacent!? This is a real war, with blood and guts and death. This isn't nightly entertainment! Thousands and thousands of people, real people, are being murdered! Communist menace? We are the menace!!"

The journalist swings toward her with his microphone at the ready, but she's turned her back and is striding off camera. She will not be a part of their game.

She walks deep into the crowd and takes aim at banal complacency. *Focus.*

She takes aim to spark action. *Click.*

Action, not words. *Wind.*

On Monday she heads to the darkroom. Lunches in the darkroom have become standard. She and Scott have settled into an odd, mutual respect. His presence soothes her. The room has become a kind of no-man's-land, a respite from her anger. She allows herself to enjoy the snatches of conversation, comes to appreciate the radio perpetually turned to CHUM-FM's eclectic programming, puts up with Scott's humming along. Sometimes he has a Dr. Pepper cooling in the washtub for her because he knows it's her favorite. He has given her some school assignments — taking photos of the drama club, the band rehearsals — and surprised her with her own set of keys.

They spend hours standing beside each other in the dark, and he leaves her alone to do her work. She's surprised at first, and then grateful. They're the same age, but she comes to think of him as a younger brother.

He's bewildered by the negatives of cows from her weekend in the country.

"Cows, princess?"

She laughs. "I'm just a little ol' country gal at heart."

But she's evasive as she makes prints from the protest. She cuts class to head to the UAE office with a new sense of purpose.

"I think I've got some great stuff from the protest." She hands Martin a coffee. "Sorry, no Danish."

He raises an eye. His face is grim. "Don't do that again."

"What, come without a Danish?" she says flirtatiously.

"Make yourself visible. Half of Nathan Phillips Square could hear you."

"You were there? I didn't see you."

"Unlike you, I was not being noticed."

She colors.

"Look, this is not a tea party. Keep your head down. Do nothing to draw attention to yourself. You were a hair's breadth away from being caught on camera."

She covers her embarrassment by spreading the photos on his desk.

He picks up the one she wants him to pick up — a shot she took of the journalist before her outburst. Martin tips the photo, looking at it from different sides.

"Huh. That's amazing. His eyes. They follow you. No matter where you look from, he catches you."

"It's something I learned at the New School. Hard to get right." A certain angle of shot, of light, and a deliberate cropping. She's never gotten it so right before. "I wanted to show how journalists are manipulating the news." All professional now.

"This is perfect. I'm doing an article about how Canadians are framing the war."

His compliment makes her impulsive. "Would you like to come to Christmas dinner?"

He looks up, surprised.

A smile starts at his lips and grows into his cheeks, his eyes, his forehead.

"That would be great. Last Christmas was my first here. It was pretty lonely. Your old lady cool with that?"

"She suggested it."

Well, that was partly true. Her mother had said she could invite a friend. She was probably expecting her to invite some waif from school. Or maybe poor Scott. "I'm making apple pie."

Martin turns the full beam of his smile on her.

"I love apple pie."

TWENTY-EIGHT

Christmas used to be filled with traditions. It has been more or less hellish since her father left.

With a tinge of cruelty, Billie asks, "Is Doris coming?"

"Doris has gone back to England. Looking for a job. Following a man. Or maybe the other way around."

Her mother has decided to create a new family for Christmas dinner — Linda and Kenny and the baby, and Henry. Surfer twins Chad and Dave fill a last-minute role of little brothers. They arrived late on December 23rd, crossing at Buffalo in sandals and shorts with no money other than the roaming $300 that the Underground Railroad provides to dodgers so they can prove to Immigration that they have cash. The same $300 circulates honorably from dodger to dodger.

Chad and Dave mystify Billie. "They look so young. All they do is play guitar." Strangled chords flop from the living room. *"Round, round, get around,"* — an awkward chord change — *"I get around, Yeah …"*

"They *are* young." Her mother is making stuffing for the first time in five years. The forest green smell of rosemary floats up from the bowl of bread cubes. "They quit high school to bum around on the beach in Santa Cruz. When Chad got drafted they decided to come up here. They said they have an aunt in Northern Ontario, a place called Cartier. But they need to make some money first, to get up there."

"They're going to job hunt in shorts and sandals? Didn't anyone tell them about Canadian winters?"

"I'll go to the Sally Ann on Boxing Day. Get them something to wear while they're here. They can't do much over the holidays anyway."

As if to spite Billie's cynicism, there are perfect fat snowflakes making mounds on bare tree limbs. The city looks like a Christmas card, and each guest arrives stamping boots and remarking on the cold, and the beauty. The early darkness sets in and the kitchen warms with the intoxicating, rich smell of roast chicken.

It's false, like a plastic Christmas tree. But it will be the last time I have to do this.

Linda sits on the floor playing patty-cake with the baby, timed to the stumbling chords.

"Tell the teacher we're surfin', Surfin' U.S.A."

Henry peels potatoes, joining in on the choruses. Kenny nurses a beer.

Her mother presides over it all, stirring gravy. She's transformed the kitchen from chaos to elegant bohemian dining. The picnic table has been pulled out diagonally and is covered in a linen tablecloth that belonged to a grandmother Billie has never met. Her mother's brass candlesticks, which always remind Billie of a weapon in Clue, are gleaming in the light of wine-colored tapers. These heirlooms, such as they are, look anachronistic — a word she just learned in English class. Anachronism: from the Greek. A misplacing or error in the order of time.

A perfect word for so many reasons.

Billie's pie is sitting in the washing machine. There wasn't another surface to put it on. Bits of crust have fallen off, to be mixed with the next batch of clothes. She doesn't admit she enjoyed making it, not even to herself.

Martin is late. Part of her hopes he won't come. She's a different person with him, more of who she really is. Billie Taylor, photographer, fighting to end the war. Here she's still decorated with a tinge of little Missy. The last bits that she can't seem to throw off.

The baby claps as the song ends, surprising everyone into laughter. Billie's mother turns, gravy spoon in one hand, question mark in the other.

"Dinner's ready. Should we wait for Martin?"

"No. He'll get here when he does."

Bowls are brought to the table. Henry carves. Platters are dispersed. Billie's senses are reeling. It's more food than she's seen in a long time.

Places are taken. An intake of breath. A moment of silence.

Her mother raises her glass. "Bless what there is for being."

Auden's grace. Their family grace. She hasn't heard it since she was little. When they were a real family. When smiles were between the three of them.

Her bitter heart clenches. She takes a gulp of Chad and Dave's sour Gallo wine. She doesn't need this fake family.

Her mother beams at everyone. "And thank you all for being here. It's the first Canadian Christmas for all of us." *First and only,* thinks Billie. "I think it would be nice if we went around the table and said what we are thankful for. I know it isn't Thanksgiving, but I think it would be nice."

God, her mother can be so embarrassing. The acid sweetness of the cranberry sauce catches in the back of Billie's throat. She suddenly sees this postcard Christmas for what it is — a bourgeois embarrassment.

"Well." Henry spreads his warmth around the table. "I'm sure thankful for my job. You were right, Jean, working at the school is incredibly rewarding. Those kids are so creative! We're making a play together about world peace. I can't believe I get paid to go to work."

Kenny looks awkward. "Well, I guess I'm thankful for Linda here. She didn't have to come. She could have stayed home with her folks. But she stayed with me."

"Oh, you silly. As if I would have let you go without me. Well, I'm real thankful for our nice apartment, and the great playgroup Joey is in. Real nice people."

"We were going to have a big beach bonfire for Christmas. I still can't believe we aren't there." Chad or Dave looks close to tears. "But I'm thankful for this dinner, and for meeting you guys."

"And I'm thankful we aren't trying to do a bonfire outside in the snow!" Chad or Dave laughs.

Billie locks her jaw, trying not to scream at their trite little thankfulnesses, knowing that if her mother pushes her to speak, she'll say something they'll both regret — when a noise in the hall makes her look up.

"The front door was open." Martin stands grinning in the doorway. "Wow, this looks fantastic!"

A strained giggle escapes from Billie. She tries to sound both casual and in control. "This is Martin."

Martin slides into the empty place. He mounds food onto his plate as introductions are made.

"I can't remember the last time I sat down to a home-cooked meal!"

He laughs and a bit of dressing escapes.

Billie realizes he's stoned. Very stoned.

"*The Exile* takes a lot of work, and I can't take time off very often. It's a real lifeline for people and that makes it really important to keep bringing it out. We only started it in October, but I can tell you it is making a real difference." He gestures to the twins in their beach gear. "We've got great, useful articles about how to survive in Canada. You'll really need that. I was just finishing up a story about how to scam the TTC and get free subway rides with old transfers!"

The twins look mystified. Henry's head comes up. "I'm not sure I agree with that. It costs money to run a transit system. And this one is really clean, and pretty efficient. I've even seen carpets in some of the subway cars."

"Oh, come on, man. These guys aren't gonna miss a few fares. And most dodgers," — he looks over Henry's tailored shirt " — most dodgers are really broke. Hey, we've even got a translation column. So you can understand Canadianese." He laughs and she sees mashed carrots between his teeth. "We've got to learn more about these people so we can get through to them. Help them see what's going on around them."

"Get through to them?" Henry has quietly put his knife and fork down.

"Canadians don't get it. They think the protests and the illegal border crossing are about Vietnam."

"Isn't it? And who said anything about illegal immigration? The Canadian government is giving us a pass, allowing us in as long as we aren't criminals."

"Yeah, well there are a lot of folks who can't get in, a lot of deserters who can't get that nice status card." Martin gesticulates wildly with his knife, the blade swooping dangerously in front of their faces. "Vietnam is a symptom. But it's about injustice everywhere. The root cause is imperialism. Imperialism and capitalism are the evils that have killed the American dream. Canada's just as bad."

Billie realizes she's a bystander to an approaching head-on collision.

"Canucks are so high and mighty. They think they're above all this. It's our job to get them to see the war machine for what it is — a money-grubbing capitalist plot. But we're going to make them join us in the fight against the imperialist bastards. We're going to make *sure* they do!"

Billie stands so quickly she almost falls backward off the bench. "Would anyone like some pie?"

Her mother is an ice statue. Henry takes over gathering plates. "My fighting days are over. I'm happy to be here. Thankful."

Martin points at Henry with his knife. "You are as much of the problem as they are, Hank. Hey, Billie, you got any beer?"

Chad/Dave's big frown has formed itself into a question. "Do you really think the Canadians are to blame?"

"All imperialists are to blame. Canadians, Americans, all of them. The system needs an overhaul. We've got to tear it down, break it apart before we can rebuild it."

"I'd be happy just to be able to go home again." Kenny's voice sounds as though he is down a deep well. "Even just for a visit."

"But there's no Canadian draft, right?" Dave/Chad's smooth face works at showing a worry line between his eyebrows.

"Ice cream?" Billie's voice is manic.

Martin clangs his empty glass on the table. "Did you see Billie's photos in *The Exile*?"

The room is suddenly silent. She thinks maybe this is what the eye of a hurricane feels like, when the winds are swirling around you but it is deadly calm in the center. You know the hurricane will keep moving and the winds will sweep you off at any minute.

"Billie has photos in your paper?" Her mother turns to her. "You didn't tell me." Billie hears the tri-tone of hurt, accusation and anger.

"They're great. She's got a fabulous eye."

"She took our picture, didn't you, Billie? She sent it back home for us. To let them know we're okay."

Chad and Dave jump up at the same time. "Will you take ours, too?"

"That's a great idea," Martin says, as though he's the one who thought of it. "A group portrait. Christmas in Canada. Put it in *The Exile*. Show people that we're surviving. That it's not all bad up here. Great idea."

"I'm not sure," says Kenny slowly. "I'm not sure it's a good idea to have our pictures in the paper."

"It's okay, man. I get it. No names. And our printer's really lousy so no one will be able to identify you. Just a happy party of strangers in a strange land."

And because it might get them out of the nightmare of this dinner, Billie stages a group portrait with everyone positioned in front of the table, the detritus of the meal, the dripping candles. Linda sitting with Joey on her knee, Kenny's arm protectively around her shoulders, looking to the side. Henry quiet and thoughtful. Dave and Chad bewildered bookends. At Martin's insistence, her mother is in the center, seated, her face a mask of granite, while he stands behind her, grinning as though this occasion was all his doing.

"Get your timer! So you can be in it, too."

She shakes her head. She is the person behind the camera. "My timer's broken. Breathe in. And again." This is not a night she wants to remember. Two worlds colliding into each other, breaking everything apart.

The evening can't end soon enough. Kenny and Linda drive Henry home. When it's clear there is no more beer, Martin stumbles out into the night. The twins decamp to their bed in the dining room. Lyrics swirl with the soapy dishwater.

Call for the Captain ashore

Let me go home …

"How could you?" her mother growls softly.

"He's a friend. He has opinions." She carefully pushes the drying cloth into the wine glass.

"What did he mean when he said, 'We're going to make Canadians join us'? Are you part of that? What is going on?"

"Nothing." Billie knows Martin wouldn't have said it if he hadn't been stoned. *We have to stay invisible.* She needs to divert her mother from the truth. "He's angry, that's all. We're all angry. You should be angry, too!"

"Don't tell me what I should and shouldn't feel. The man is a mess. He was stoned out of his gourd."

"So? The twins got drunk. What's the big deal?"

Her mother spins around so quickly that Billie clutches the glass against her to keep it from flying across the room.

"*What's the big deal?* Don't you remember what it was like? Don't you remember your father like that night after night after night? I've brought you here for a new life, a fresh start and you climb into bed with the past, with a mess, with a disaster. Jesus, Billie!" Her mother's face is shattered. "I can't do this again. I can't have another junkie in my life!"

Any lingering Christmas compassion has vanished. Billie latches onto anger. "Martin is not a junkie! He just smokes up. Just some grass. Everybody smokes grass. And I'm not sleeping with him!"

Her mother is silent stone.

"And what the hell would it matter if I was? This is *my* life! Martin is the only friend I have in this city. He's a friend. I'm not sleeping with him. And yes I do remember what it was like, but I can't believe you brought Pops into this! This has nothing to do with Pops and it has nothing to do with you!"

And she storms out of the kitchen with nowhere to go except her bedroom, where even the pillow can't drown out the endless repetition of the Sloop John B.

Let me go home . . .

TWENTY-NINE

She works the New Year's shift at the Mynah Bird and starts back at Jarvis Collegiate with a massive hangover.

It's 1969. She hasn't heard from Martin since the horror of Christmas. She no longer has to work at being invisible. It comes quite naturally. The ice, snow and cold have driven everyone inside. She wonders if winter is the reason why revolutions usually happen in hot countries.

Bitter January becomes ice-encrusted February. At the Mynah Bird, Cheryl, Harry, the strippers and the regulars cling together, trying to keep each other in good humor. But Billie can't find anything to feel good about. She watches the tips dwindle, her savings account flatline. Her eighteenth birthday comes and goes. Her mother warily gives her a new shutter-release cord for her camera. She feels sorry for herself and rereads *The Spice-Box of Earth*.

But the first of March brings an unexpected warmth that thaws the world. She trades her heavy wool tights for fishnets and struts to work, clicking her boot heels on the sidewalk.

"Goin' my way?" A familiar voice behind her makes her spin. Martin's smile lights up the night, but he speaks quietly as he is passing her. "Jack's in town. Wants to see you. Tomorrow night. You don't work Sundays, right?"

She lets out a breath she didn't realize she was holding.

"Ashram Lounge. Eight o'clock."

He picks up his pace, passes her and is gone.

"I'm going to a movie with a guy I met at school. Charlie. *The Love Bug*. Some silly thing about a Beetle. No, not the band. A car. We might go for coffee after. I might be late."

It isn't a lie. It's an alternate reality. *This is the life I might be leading. This is the Billie you want.*

And she's out the door into the dark, navigating sidewalks of rock-hard ice and frozen gray slush, walking the five blocks to Rochdale, where the biker bouncer nods her in. She takes the elevator to the seventh floor and knocks on the locked door.

A young kid, barely a teenager, opens the door and peers at her warily from under a mop of greasy hair.

"I'm here to see Martin." The lounge is quiet, the television silent.

The boy scowls. "Down the hall. Last unit."

Billie notes a small scale on the table and feels the boy's

suspicious eyes drill into her back as she heads down the hallway. He doesn't seem old enough to smoke, let alone be a dealer.

At the end of the hall, Billie knocks on the door.

She stands uncertain in the hallway and hears a lock click. The door opens just enough for Martin to propel her inside, close the door and turn the lock.

Jack sits cross-legged, Buddha-like on the desk, his thick beard obscuring expression, his eyes inscrutable. Vivien, her legs curled under her on the bed, looks shriveled, like something found under the winter snow melt. Her arms are rail thin and her skin a shade of pewter. But her eyes are flames.

There are no smiles. But Billie feels an immediate sense of belonging, of emerging from hibernation to find her family. They are a team and she matters.

On the desk, spread out in front of Jack's feet, is a carpet of photographs. Jeweled shades of green jungle. Lush. Opulent. She knows they are spread out for her to look at, and her photographer's eye can't resist.

"Viv's ex took them. The rainforests of Vietnam."

Billie's eyes flick to Vivien. *Ted's a mess. 'Nam fried him.*

"They're beautiful," she says, and means it. The quality and the images. She had no idea that Vietnam was such a jungle paradise.

"He took these six months later."

Jack shuffles a second layer of photos over the first. Gray wasted landscapes. Scorched trees.

The contrast is mesmerizing. Her eyes slide between Before to the unrecognizable After.

"Agent Orange," says Jack, "defoliates the forest. It burns, poisons and kills everything it touches." He turns to Billie.

"The recipe was developed by Columbia."

She looks at him. "I know. It's one of the reasons Dan left school."

What do you do when you know the truth? He had enlisted. She had done nothing.

Jack flips over another handful of photos.

A beautiful boy is sitting on a pillow on the ground, his arms and legs wizened stumps. A girl, her head cocked to the side, stares at the camera, the top half of her head completely deformed, mangled, melted. A face melted beyond recognition, with only two dots to suggest nostrils. A boy with bulging eyes and a pointed head like a space alien. A tiny baby with a head too impossibly huge to lift from a stained pillow.

Pictures of monsters. Pictures of indescribable horror.

"Agent Orange deforms babies."

Billie closes her eyes, but the images are burned into her brain. She cannot unsee them. This is so much worse than what she'd imagined.

There is a pause as she tries to swallow.

"Agent Orange," continues Jack, "is made in a factory in Elmira, Ontario. Just outside of Waterloo."

Her eyes snap open.

"The recipe came from Columbia, but it's made in Canada." His eyes bore into hers. "Made in Canada, near the farmhouse."

The room is dead calm. From down the hall she hears the blare of Jefferson Airplane on a stereo.

When the truth is found —

to be —

lies …

"The Uniroyal Chemical Company makes Agent Orange in Elmira, Ontario, and ships it at night on an old rail line. They ship it from Elmira through a little Mennonite town called St. Jacobs, to Waterloo, to the US. To Vietnam. They make Agent Orange, and Agent Orange does this to unborn children."

He hands her the photos, gives her the monstrous children to hold.

She looks directly at Jack. His eyes pull her to the truth.

"We can stop this."

And she knows that she will do anything to stop this.

"There's a weak point on the rail line. A bridge outside of St. Jacobs. If the bridge is gone, they can't ship the chemical. If the bridge is gone, there will be no more babies born looking like this. Simple."

If the bridge is gone …

She can't look at the pictures. She must look at the pictures.

"I talked to people. In Montreal. The FLQ. You heard about that bomb in the stock exchange? That was only part of their plan. They're fighting to liberate themselves from the English oppressors and they know their stuff. They gave me a copy of this." Jack flourishes a newspaper from his worn canvas pack, the *San Francisco Express Times*, and casually flips it open.

The headline on the front page: "How to Make Your Own Bomb."

"Basic stuff." Jack is pointing at the line drawing of a bag of fertilizer, a stick of dynamite, and wires to a blasting cap and a clock.

"Fertilizer. Dynamite. Blasting caps. A clock. As the guys in Montreal said, all available at your local country hardware store."

Her eyes dart from the bomb to the monster children and back again.

"But you've got to do it right. They made some mistakes in Montreal. Blew up more than they needed to and some people got hurt. We need to study the bridge. Get some engineering advice so we know where to put the dynamite and fertilizer. We need to get it right. Take some photos."

Focus. *Take some photos ...*

"I've got a friend in engineering at University of Waterloo. We'll show him some pictures of the bridge. Find the weak spot in the construction. Everything has its weak spot. The weak spot will show up in your pictures."

Click. *Your pictures.*

The flame of a match flares and Jack sucks it into his cigarette. She hears the pull of his lungs and smells the sulfur and dust. She looks around at the three of them.

"The time for talk is over." Martin is leaning on the doorframe.

"Once you see the lie for what it is, you can't run away from it." Vivien's voice is clear, unemotional.

The air is thin.

And just like winding her camera, she nods.

This is what she's wanted. To be part of a plan. To belong to this new family.

Jack hops down from the desk. Puts his hand on her shoulder. "We'll go to the farm. Once the ground thaws."

But the moment is shattered by heavy feet racing down the hall and a bang on the door.

"COPS OUT FRONT!" a voice yells from the hall.

"SHIT."

"IT'S A RAID!"

"Shit, shit, shit, shit, shit!"

"It's okay, man." Martin reaches a hand toward Jack. "They can't get in here. We've got Angels on our side," he says with a grin.

But Jack is moving double speed, frantically sweeping the photos together. He thrusts the article at Martin.

How to Make Your Own Bomb.

"Memorize this article, then burn it."

He shoves all the photos at Billie. "Put these down your pants."

She stares at them as though they are the poison.

He claps his hands. "NOW!" He grabs at his bag, catching only the strap. It skitters across the desk and onto the floor with a thud.

A gun falls out.

Jack sweeps it back into the bag without comment and turns to Martin. "Is there another way out?"

Billie pushes the hideous photos between her pants and her bare skin.

A gun.

"The fire escape at the other end of the building." Martin's voice is matter-of-fact. "You have to go through the lounge, past the elevator and down the west hallway. Past the Aphrodite Units. The west fire escape opens onto Huron Street."

"Okay. The car's on Huron. Viv and I are going back to Waterloo." Jack zeroes in on Billie. "When you get out of here, tear up the photos. Put the pieces in a public garbage can." The sharp edges of the photo paper tear at the skin of her belly. She tugs at her zipper to secure the stack in place. She looks at his bag. At the gun weight of it.

Jack turns on Martin and looks at Billie. "Do not be seen together."

He crosses the room in two steps and cautiously opens the door.

"Billie — come with us."

And faster than thought, he grabs her arm and she is through the lounge, past the elevators, down a hall of open doors — doors to small apartments where heads briefly surface, then withdraw, turtle-like. She races behind Jack and Viv, through a fire door, down the stairs, pounding down seven flights to a steel door that says Exit.

"They aren't looking for you. Go out and see if it's clear."

She hasn't caught her breath before she stretches her head out into the dark cool of the side street. She can hear yelling on the other side of the building. But she looks along Huron Street and sees only a startled squirrel fling himself into a low-hanging tree branch and vanish into the overgrowth.

She turns back to the doorway. She nods.

The two bodies streak past her like ghosts.

The door locks with a soft clunk. She's alone as she hears the distant cough of a car that needs a new muffler.

She's alone as her heart rate slows. She's alone as she turns into the alley behind Rochdale, her hands instinctively protecting the wad of photos at her belly.

Her temples pound with every boot step as she navigates the icy streets to a dark park blocks away. A child's swing rocks emptily in the night wind. A large trash can sits under a tree.

She tears the photos, and eyes, hands, limbless bodies, lush jungles and scorched trees mix with used Styrofoam cups in the deserted garbage can.

We'll go to the farm.

She'll take her father's Hasselblad.

THIRTY

She dates the imaginary Charlie and drops false bread crumbs for her mother. She becomes invisible as she moves through school, going to classes, writing exams, taking photographs of nail-biting chess tournaments and toga-clad thespians intoning about Caesar and the Ides of March.

The images of the monster babies burn in her brain. The memory of the glossy photos coats her belly.

It's a Saturday in mid-March when Martin sits down at the bar of the Mynah Bird. He orders a coffee. Like a stranger.

As she sets down the fat cup and saucer, he quietly says, "Tomorrow."

She slides a cream pitcher in front of him.

"Wait in the bus station at Bay and Dundas. Three o'clock. Pack for a couple of days."

"Charlie's family invited me to their cottage for a few days for March Break. Up in a place called Honey Harbour." She's stolen the name from a couple of the drama club kids making their March Break plans.

She knows her mother is relieved at the increasing importance of Charlie in her life.

She's covered her tracks. No one will know where she is or who she is with.

She doesn't know how long they'll be gone, or what the plan is, but she is ready, the Hasselblad safe in its leather case. She's cleaned and polished it and loaded a fresh roll of film. She feels its weight like the anxious energy of a racehorse behind the starting gate. Waiting for the bang of a starter's pistol.

She waits on the hard wooden bench at the bus station. *The Wretched of the Earth* is on her lap.

She doesn't see Martin, doesn't recognize him in his horn-rimmed glasses, close-cropped hair and button-down shirt until he slides onto the bench beside her. He drops a floppy hat over the book.

"Don't advertise," he snaps.

She jams the book into her pack, embarrassed. He stands and strides across the waiting room. She rushes across the dingy linoleum to catch up with him, unsure of what to do with the hat.

"The car's around the corner. We'll pick up some egg rolls and chow mein for dinner."

"I thought we were taking a bus."

He doesn't look at her. "Just a neutral place to meet up."

She flaps the hat at him, with a question.

"Put it on."

The large brim flops over her eyes. She notices his mouth tighten as he controls a laugh. "Jack is a master of disguise. It suits you not at all."

The farm is much as she remembers it, although this time the snow is melting, not falling. The cattle are, she swears, standing in the same spot. Vivien, like Martin, has changed her hair. The dark brunette bob is nondescript.

She's never seen Jack without a beard. She didn't realize he was keeping a couple of chins underneath it.

"It's a disguise I can grow out of quickly." He grins as he rips open the bag of chow mein and egg rolls.

Billie slides the paper off a pair of chopsticks and delicately picks up a slithery bean sprout.

Jack watches her. "Nice."

"My father taught me when I was little."

"You were raised right, with respect for the teachings of Chairman Mao."

Despite herself, she laughs. "They're just chopsticks."

"From chopsticks to Hanoi!"

Candles are lit. Martin turns on an old record player, like the kind her father used to have. Applause and audience sounds fill the room, and she feels surrounded by thousands of people. Guitars pull a story together. Janis Joplin growls an old song.

Summertime
And the livin' is easy ...

Jack starts, as though picking up from the middle of a speech.

"The US government knows the truth about Agent Orange. They say it's okay because they are spraying it on the enemy. But those rice paddies they're spraying feed civilians. They are *deliberately* deforming unborn children. They're committing a clear war crime according to the Geneva Convention, and *no one* is stopping them."

The candles glow. She trails the last bean sprout through the sauce.

"Canadians think they're not in this war. But they supply the poison. They're accomplices to murder."

She puts down her bowl. Martin rests his hand gently on her knee.

Warriors in the wilderness, gathered around the fire.

"They say they're gonna bomb Vietnam back to the stone age." Jack smiles. "But we're gonna bomb *them* back to the stone age."

Vivien is holding herself and gently rocking. "We've got to save the children."

"We're going do something they can't forget, can't ignore." Jack exhales the blue fog and passes the hash along. "It's gonna mean something. *We're* gonna mean something."

THIRTY-ONE

"These overalls should fit you. God, they could fit two of you!"

Vivien holds out some dirty overalls. Billie thinks of Mr. Green Jeans on Captain Kangaroo. He's the only person she's ever seen wearing overalls.

"And to complete the ensemble …" Vivien hands her a red plaid flannel shirt.

"You're kidding."

Vivien's mouth curves up in a half smile. "We'll braid your hair, too. That way you won't need to cut it."

And so she is transformed from Miranda Billie Taylor to

Cathy Brown, newly moved to the country, renting out the old Murphy place.

"If anyone wanted to, they could easily trace the Murphy place to Professor McFadden. But he's never heard of Cathy Brown, let alone Billie Taylor, so it should stop there. Worse comes to worst he'll probably say some hippies stole his keys and broke into his place. Which wouldn't be far off."

"Why are Martin and I buying the dynamite?"

"Because we need it to blow up the bridge." Jack's impatience cuts through his pacing.

"No, I mean why us?"

"Because of your young innocent look. And your accent."

"My accent?"

"You don't sound American," says Vivien. "Foreign, but not American. The rest of us would be spotted in a minute. But you help Martin to pass."

Jack squares off in front of her, a general giving commands. "Remember, pick up some basic things. Make the dynamite incidental. Oh, and get a jug of maple syrup. About a gallon. Apparently it makes a great conductor."

The radio is playing the noon news when they enter the general store in Sebringville. The "Farm Report." Something about hog prices. The body count here is strictly in pork.

Rough wooden floors creak with every step. Billie's on high alert as she and Martin negotiate the warren of shelves. She's aware of every tromping step in her oversized rubber boots. She picks out a new enamel washbasin and a bar of Sunlight soap. Martin selects blue checked handkerchiefs, thick red socks, a handful of two-inch nails and a mousetrap.

Random items that look purposeful laid out on the scuffed wooden counter.

A red-headed pimply-faced boy scoops the nails into a small paper bag. His hands pause beside the huge cash register. "That be all?"

"Maple syrup?" Billie smiles flirtatiously at the teenager to cover her nervousness. He turns pink. "Have you got a gallon of maple syrup?"

"Over there." He points. She can hear him trying to control the crack in his voice.

She heads down the aisle. Takes a deep breath. "Oh, and what about the dynamite, honey?" she says breezily, aiming her voice back to Martin. "I thought you were gonna blast that huge boulder out of the hay field." Her legs are shaking. The lines are rehearsed. They sound incredibly fake. She's sure the boy will know she's lying. She returns to the counter with the maple syrup and a smile.

"Oh, yeah." Martin mumbles. "A box of dynamite. Twelve should do it."

The boy looks up from where he's been writing up their purchases. "Um, ah … I'm supposed to ask to see your certificate. You know. For the course? In handling dynamite?" His voice is full of apology.

Billie freezes. Certificate? Course? She watches Martin pull out his wallet and rifle through it.

"Dang," he says softly. (*Dang?* thinks Billie.) "I musta left it back at the house. We'll hafta come back for all of this stuff later." He turns away from the counter.

Billie looks at the boy. His face goes scarlet from the tips of his ears to his throat.

"Naw, it's okay," he says, shrugging. "I'll get it for you. Just one of those stupid government rules, eh?"

They all have a little laugh.

"Thanks so much." She beams at him. Her breath is coming in short gasps.

The boy heads to a back shelf, somewhere out of sight. "You needing some blasting caps?" he calls from the depths of the shop.

Martin laughs. "Wouldn't be much good without 'em, would it?"

The boy emerges from behind the shelves with a small cardboard box that he places carefully on the counter.

"Can't be too careful with this stuff," he says. "Make sure you keep it dry. Here's your caps. Don't bounce them around. Knock them and they'll go off. Boom!"

Martin pays for their purchases and lifts the caps and dynamite sticks gently off the counter. Billie feels her smile is maniacal as she scoops up the bag of goods.

"Well, thanks again." They head to the door.

Her hand is on the latch when his voice stops her.

"So where y'all from?"

She turns. *Cathy Brown, renting the old Murphy place*, she repeats in her head. Her mouth opens. "Well …"

"You from England? You sound like you're from England."

She tries to make her mouth smile but her lips are rigid against her teeth. She nods slowly.

"Yeah, I thought so." The boy looks proud of himself. "My grandmother was from England. Y'all have a good day."

They are a mile away before her laughter bursts the bubble of raw nerves.

At the farm, she slurps spoonfuls of Vivien's thin minestrone soup. Their purchases are arranged on the floor of the farm's cold, fly-filled living room. While they were in Sebringville, Jack and Vivien drove to Mitchell to buy thin yellow electrical wire and bags of nitrogen corn fertilizer.

"Burpee's Feed and Seed said it was a bit early for fertilizer. Woman said there's a late snowstorm coming in next week. I laughed and said I wouldn't be putting it on until at least May. I just wanted to be all prepared. My Girl Scout training, I said."

"Well, that's true." Jack helps himself to the last of the soup. "We won't be putting it out until May. When they celebrate a dead queen. Victoria Day weekend. It'll make your crops explode!" His laugh is oversized. He bends back the cap of a bottle of Black Label. "We'll give these country bumpkins a hell of a holiday to remember."

Her beer tastes sharp, but she's giddy with relief. She could drink a dozen beers and not get drunk.

"We've got to store the stuff until then. Spread it out. We'll leave the fertilizer and maple syrup here. Take the wires to Viv's. The caps and dynamite to Billie's."

"What?" She almost spits out her beer. "Why my place?"

"Process of elimination. Can't take it to Rochdale. Some freak would find it and blow the whole building up!"

She turns to Jack. "What about you?"

"I'm couch surfing." He shrugs.

"What about Vivien? Why can't you take it? I'll take the wires."

"The basement of my rooming house floods," Vivien explains patiently. "Dynamite and caps have to stay dry."

Billie looks at them, but no one is looking at her. Jack

runs his finger along the inside of his bowl to catch the last tastes of soup.

"Just make sure you're careful with the caps. They're sensitive. Bang them and they go off."

They've discussed this, drawn straws, given her the short one.

She squares her shoulders. The good soldier. "Right."

Martin casually kisses her on the top of her head as he goes to the record player. Vivien's tongue glides along the edge of a cigarette paper. She twists a joint tight, puts it in her mouth and drags it out to offer it to Jack. A guitar solo rips into the room.

Jack passes the joint to Martin. He pulls an envelope from his bag. A bass guitar underscores his movements.

"I got a letter from 'Nam. The kind of thing the nightly news doesn't report. Consider this your bedtime story, children. With Agent Orange as a bit player."

Billie's lips feel the cool bulge of the neck of her beer bottle as he begins.

"You can't run." Jack reads slowly, dispassionately, letting the words do their work.

"Agent Orange has stripped the trees so there's nowhere to hide. We watched when the bombs started falling. Graceful. Slow. End over end. Silent. All of the buzzing, humming insects just waiting and watching. It was beautiful in the center of that silence. When the earth heaved me into the sky it was a silent ballet."

Billie's hand is tight around the stubby cold brown bottle.

"When I hit the ground there was a leg in my lap. It wasn't mine. I checked. There were a lot of bodies. But I couldn't find one missing a leg. Should I bury a leg without a body? But maybe everyone needs an extra. A leg up, a leg over, a leg to stand on,

break a leg, you're pulling my leg … If only they could run as fast as their legs could carry them. But you can't run."

The only sound in the room is the scratch … scratch … scratch of the record needle at the end of the record.

Jack inhales. The joint glows. Smoke pours over his chin as he exhales. "We don't want to be too close when the bridge goes up. We've gotta find the best place to stand. We need to be close enough to get a good picture to send in to the papers. Getting press on this is important. It needs to get counted. In the US, they figure there's almost one bombing a day. Collectives all over the States are choosing targets to get the most press. It doesn't mean anything if people don't know why it's happening."

Martin sucks the last bit out of the joint. "I'm writing a manifesto. To send to the press with a photo of the bridge blowing up." Vivien nods.

"Billie and I will go to the bridge in the morning." Jack turns to her, giving her the next day's orders. "You'll take structural photos for planning. Catch it in the light. We'll be back before we need to lock up here."

The next morning, the Hasselblad is in her hands. She's been waiting to use it for five years. At her touch, the viewfinder springs into action. As though it has been waiting for her, too.

The bridge stretches heavily over her. It's not a tiny wooden bridge that the Billy Goats Gruff tromp over. It's solid. Imposing. A weight she hadn't expected. Massive steel girders support a train's length of track over a wild stretch of river. A river deep enough to drown a train.

Surely a few bags of fertilizer can't bring that down.

Can they?

"We need shots of the whole span, the pylons, the footings." Jack's dancing under the bridge. "Give me close-ups showing weight-bearing. We need to know where to put the bags." Bouncing, breathless, excited. "We've only got one chance. We've got to get it right."

She looks down. Her hands are her father's hands. She aims at the span above her and adjusts her focus, the ridges of the knob turning softly, smoothly, with such delicacy, such precision. Her father's abandoned gift.

She checks her aperture and speed and looks through the crystal-clear viewfinder. The world outside the frame is gone. She focuses on the connection between vertical and horizontal and on the space between the tracks. The negative space. Her finger rests on the button beside the lens. She breathes in slowly. And she clicks.

Each movement is smooth, clean, the camera leading. The rest of the world drops away. She focuses and shoots, shoots and focuses to Jack's directions. Catching angles, girders, rivets. The camera sees the workmanship and the beauty that the railway workers took for granted. She scales the bank and shoots the view from underneath, capturing the graffiti on the concrete footing — Floyd loves Susie — while the morning releases the decomposing smell of riverbank into the early spring.

His touch makes her jump. She turns to face him. They are in the dark cavern where the footings meet the bank. A cathedral of girders.

"You wrecked the shot."

"Can you see it?" He's all sweat and spring mud and nervous energy. "See it slowly rising up, up, released like a caged bird?"

He takes a step closer. The air is thin between them.

She raises her camera.

He pushes it gently down. "You've got enough."

In the quiet, early robins call each other from the trees on either side of the river. She begins to turn away when he stops her.

"I got a letter from Dan."

"What?"

"I got a letter. From Dan. For you."

Disbelief, anger and hurt flash through her. "He's never written to me."

"He sent a letter to you, through me. From Vietnam."

"But he's not in Vietnam. He's at Fort Devens."

"No, Billie. He's been in 'Nam for six months. That letter I read last night was from him. A letter he wrote to me."

For a moment she is still.

Then her legs collapse. The cold wet of the earth soaks into her.

He pulls a yellowed paper from his pack and hands it to her.

"He sent a different one to you."

B.,

The world is filled with lies.

Too many lies.

You were right. Of course. I shouldn't have enlisted, should never have thought I could do it inside.

Nothing worked the way I thought it would.

The machine is too big. They made it easy to smile. The nightmare is papered with smiles. Each needle is filled with smiles. And snakes. Snakes with smiles.

You were before. Now is forever after.
"Cold skeletons go marching.
Each night beside my feet."
Leonard Cohen
Dan

Jack gently takes the paper from her. "The army gives out heroin like candy. It's the only way they can get through the hell." His voice is caring and soft now. "The Dan we knew is gone. A junkie."

She sees her father's feet. Yellow. Dirty. Sweat that smelled like sweet metal.

Not Dan.

She grabs at the camera, raising it in her hand to hurl it down the rail bed, but Jack is there and he grabs it.

"We're gonna do this, Billie. We're gonna do it for Dan. For Dan, for the children, for the forests — everything that is being destroyed."

He's speaking deliberately, slowly, treating her like a spooked horse under the girders and the rails. The air is filled with the decay of leaves.

"I'll light the fuse," he says, "but you'll take the picture. You'll make it happen."

Smiles. Snakes. Needles. Skeletons marching.

She opens her eyes and sees the bridge growing, heaving into the sky, a fireball blasting up, a cleansing force.

She wants to do it now. She wants to go up with it, a blaze, into the clear blue sky.

THIRTY-TWO

She needs to be alone in the darkroom. The pictures of the bridge have to be developed, but Scott can't see these.

"Jesus, can't you leave me alone for once? Doesn't it occur to you that maybe I don't want to share every minute of my life with you?"

Her anger has shocked him into silence.

"Fine, stay." She gambles. "I've got some great nude photos of my new boyfriend and some self-timed sex. Sure, stick around, pervert."

He scurries out of the darkroom. She's bought herself privacy and ignores the cost.

Stopping the war machinery is more important than delicate feelings.

The prints are good. She cuts the negatives into confetti-sized pieces and scatters them in the garbage can in the park. She carries the prints in her bag and waits. The box of dynamite sits at the bottom of her closet, buried under a mound of winter clothes. The box of caps is buried in the bottom of her dresser drawer.

She coils into herself like a spring.

Cold April, then an unseasonal heat wave in May. The patio at the Mynah Bird opens. She's sticky under her bikini when she sees Vivien's eyes flash out from under a broad, floppy hat, her hair now a mousy blond. She slips the manila envelope of prints into Viv's large straw bag. No words are said.

Her smiles are rehearsed. Her heart is wrapped around the monster children, the orphaned leg, the veins punctured with needles that take away those she loves.

Queen Victoria Day weekend. The appetite for beer is insatiable on the patio at the Mynah Bird. Martin is there in a pressed blue shirt, ordering a Labatt's Blue, handing her a bright orange two-dollar bill, saying quietly, "Put the box of dynamite on your porch tonight. Two in the morning. Be at Rochdale tomorrow. Eight p.m." She hands him some change, isn't sure how much. None of it matters anymore.

Two in the morning. The hall stair outside her mother's room squeaks but she stretches her legs beyond to the next step. She tiptoes the box of dynamite from closet to porch. Then lies sleepless in bed until she hears a car idle briefly, a trunk open and shut, and has her first dreamless sleep in weeks.

But she's slapped awake by adrenaline. She forgot to give him the caps. Nothing works without the caps. The blasting caps are at the bottom of her dresser drawer.

She'll have to carry them to Rochdale tonight. *Just make sure you're careful with the caps. They're sensitive. Bang them and they go off.* She'll have to cradle them for five blocks, without a misstep on the concrete sidewalk between her house and her future.

She loads new film in the Hasselblad. Fast speed will capture the blast. A shot of pure action. As close as she can get.

She tells her mother she's going to a movie with Charlie and she might be late. That she might stay over. She feels a slight tug as she walks away. Steel girders falling. Silent, end over end.

Nothing matters except action.

Sun slants along the length of Bloor Street as she walks to Rochdale, cradling the box. From a block away she can see Jack's face beaming in the late sun, full of purpose and excitement as he crosses in front of the lumpy statue and walks toward her.

His eyes lock onto hers like a tractor beam, pulling her forward. They are together in this moment of anticipation, of ignition, the moment where action begins and events spin outward.

But suddenly in her peripheral vision she sees a circle of blue police swarm behind him. A blue wave. A wave of snarling fury raising black clubs that he doesn't see.

She responds instinctively, just like at Columbia. In one smooth motion she sets the box at her feet, pulls out her Hasselblad, raises it, a witness, a war correspondent, and she focuses on the clubs as the wave rises and crashes and the clubs smash and Jack topples and the clubs rise again.

She is there with her camera — *focus, click, wind.* Her breath is clear — *focus, click, wind, focus* — focused on her viewfinder, focused until she sees a cop coming toward her, reaching for her camera.

And in that moment the sound comes back on and the air is filled with screams and thuds and suddenly her mind wakes up with the cold certainty of what is going to happen.

The blasting caps at her feet.

His heavy feet, heavy boots will kick the box. *Bang them and they'll go off.* Her legs blown off, her belly split open, an explosion that will tear through her and her legs will rain from the sky and she will be on the front page of the war and time stretches and she knows that the bridge won't go up, that it's her going up and not coming down, the children not coming down, the war never ending —

It is not supposed to be like this! This isn't the story!

— and his boot is moving and her bag is a breath away and it only takes only an instant to die when a biker guard, an Angel, cuts between her and the boot, deflecting the cop, giving her the slightest fraction of a moment to scoop up the box — carefully, oh my god, carefully like cradling a baby, scoop up the box with the blasting caps as her guardian angel stops the heavy feet, and she is instantly invisible in the crowd and she is on a new path.

A new path that she can walk on with her own legs, legs not blown off, a path away from the screams, a path where there is nothing to connect her to the man being beaten on the ground, I don't know him, I've never seen him, I live at home with my mother just the two of us and her mind is blank except for the caps, the fucking blasting caps what the fuck should she do with them no one has prepared her for this and she is walking and shaking but she has to keep the caps still SHE HAS TO KEEP THE CAPS STILL she doesn't want to die she wants to have something to live for and she has to get rid of the caps so she walks the length of the city as far from the man and the cops and the dynamite in a room in the Ashram, as far as she can go, the length of the city and she is at the water and the deserted wharf at the end of the city where there is water and she must not get the caps wet or they won't work, they won't work when they are wet and she gingerly tips the small box into the lake as gently as if she was drowning a baby.

She turns her key. Soft lights glow. TV lights flicker.

Casablanca is on the television. Her father took her to see it in a theater on 42nd Street for her tenth birthday. "The shadow under Bergman's hat is sheer poetry," he'd said. No one else has that memory. It is hers, like his camera. One of the few things he's left her. From the time before bombs and legs falling from the sky, from the time before.

"Billie?"

She chokes and tells the last lie. "Charlie and I broke up."

And her mother is putting a mug of sweet tea in her hands and a blanket over her shaking legs, placing a box of Kleenex in front of her and she is a little girl, a little girl who doesn't want to be dead, who doesn't want her father to have left or her boyfriend to be a junkie or monster children to be born and she is crying, finally crying while her mother holds her.

THIRTY-THREE

Days pass. There is nothing in the papers. Nothing about Jack, nothing about the rail bridge outside of Elmira, over which, presumably, Agent Orange continues to travel.

She carefully times her visit to the darkroom. Scott is still scarce as a scolded child. She develops the film, replaying the moment over and over. Her prints reveal a violent truth, a war zone on the streets of Toronto. The war on her, her friends, her generation. The pictures that tell a story not of a bridge, but of a democracy blowing up.

This is the story she wants to tell. This is the story she wants to be alive to tell.

But like all stories, it carries the traces of a storyteller. The story must be told, but she must remain invisible, leave no trail.

She places the prints in an envelope. In the still night, she quietly navigates the dark streets down to the UAE office. She leaves the envelope of prints in the mailbox. Unsigned.

She takes her first deep breath. She has left no trace. The story is no longer hers to tell.

She apologizes to Scott with Twinkies and a Hires Root Beer.

She lets her mother take her shopping.

Her eyes see everything during her shift at the Mynah Bird, but there is nothing to see. No Jack. No Martin. No Vivien.

A car backfires and she crashes against a table, spilling a full jug of beer. She tries to turn it into a joke about her period putting her off balance.

"You look like you haven't slept in a week," says Cheryl. "Go home and come back when you can carry a tray."

But the nights pummel her with images. Melted children. Clubs smashing. Limbs blown sky-high.

She limps into the first Saturday of June. The kitchen is filled with the smell of baking muffins. The washing machine is chugging in the corner. A note from her mother reads, *Gone to get milk.* A folded newspaper is squashed between the cups and jars of jams on the table. She opens it from habit.

Police Brutality in Toronto?

The headline sits on top of a familiar photo of blurred uniforms, clubs raised, grimaced faces snarling over a hunched man.

Her photo. The best of the lot.

She quickly scans for a credit. *Photograph courtesy of the Union of American Exiles. Anonymous.*

Her photo. Front page. Fear and pride churn. She scans the article.

Jack Grogan, 22, was arrested on three counts of drug possession, trafficking of narcotics, possession of a firearm and conspiracy to commit acts of violence. He has been deported to the United States where he is awaiting trial. When questioned by reporters about the aggressive police response, Chief of Police Bill Green defended the actions. "We have been investigating a terror group operating out of Rochdale College. These kids are coming up from the United States and inciting violence." Is this a picture of democracy? Has the war on our youth come to Toronto? In the opinion of this writer, photographs do not lie. The mayor's proposal to establish a commission of inquiry into excessive police violence is timely.

Photographs do not lie. They change hearts and minds. They change the world.

She thinks of the photograph that she did not take — the photograph of a bridge arcing skyward. A photograph trying to make news, not framing truth.

She hears her mother's key in the lock of the front door and slides the paper back on the table. Her mother, who has smiled more in the past week than in the past five years, who arrives in the kitchen with the warm spring day in her hair, who hugs her and forgives what she doesn't know.

Her summer hours at the Mynah Bird include busy sun-drenched patio afternoons, so busy that it takes a slow turn of the earth before she recognizes Martin's voice from under a beard and a broad-rimmed felt hat.

"Coffee."

She flits between customers, and he orders apple strudel.

His voice floats up to her as she puts down his plate and cup, not making eye contact. "I'm hitching to Van. Might start a paper out there. Viv's coming, too. We've already contacted the Vancouver Committee to Aid War Objectors. Hoping we can do some work with them."

She allows her eyes to quickly scan his face. His eyes focus on his coffee. The spoon clicks in the cup. His voice is mostly air. "He'll spend a long time in jail. Most of his life."

She moves away and through the patio. She thinks of Jack eating oatmeal. Jack and Dan. Both destroyed by the war. Both destroyed because they wanted to make a difference. They were willing to die for it.

Carrying the weight of those blasting caps changed her path. Her "moment of glory" as Jack would have said, is past. In *her* story, her hands hold a Hasselblad. In *her* story, she can work to make the world a better place as a photojournalist.

In *her* story, she can tell the story. Not be the story.

She circles back to Martin. "Can I get you anything else?" She juts out her hip, as she does with all customers.

He smiles at her. "I'll send you my address when I'm set up. Maybe you could come out."

"Looks like I'll finish high school here. Grade thirteen." She makes a face as she makes change.

"It is a *damn* good photo," he whispers as he pays the bill.

He leaves a small tip and is gone.

When the whirly brass doorbell rings in late August, Billie assumes it's another draft dodger. She opens the door and looks at the ragged, overgrown brushcut, the greasy, pale skin.

Deserter, she thinks. Definitely deserter.

He is framed by the ragged snowballs of the giant hydrangeas beside the front porch.

"Billie."

Her eyes search and she sees chiseled cheekbones under the rough stubble. Intense electric-blue eyes, bloodshot and yellow.

It has been a year since she has seen him. It has been a lifetime.

Beside him under the gentle curve of his arm is a woman. Her dark eyes flash from underneath a fringe of shiny black hair. Her hands rest protectively on her stretched pregnant belly.

He's sweating the recognizable smell of a junkie. She watches him concentrate to make sentences. Her mother has come to the door, is standing beside her. Billie feels her fear. *I can't have another junkie in my life ...*

He's strung out, but making an effort. For Billie. For her mother. And for the pregnant Vietnamese girl by his side.

"Tuyen needs a family. Everything in her village was destroyed." His eyes plead. "There was nowhere else to take her."

He looks into her mother's eyes. "I won't stay."

He looks into Tuyen's eyes. "*Bạn có thể tin tưởng họ,*" he says.

His voice familiar, so close. And half the world away.

"You can trust them," he says.

He peels her fingers from his arm. His hand rests briefly on her belly. Her nose is flared like a spooked horse.

"*Bạn có thể tin tưởng họ.*"

Billie's mother slowly, softly, places her hand on Tuyen's tight fist.

A life story plays out in front of Billie. Abandonment. Betrayal. A war zone of unspeakable horror. She knows that not everyone can be saved. But that those who can, must be.

EPILOGUE

She flips over the Hasselblad and screws in the plate for the tripod. Her mother cried when Billie showed her the camera. Then they both cried. It has taken six years for them to cry together over the loss of her father.

The house is filled with the smell of sweet creamy bánh pia. It is Tuyen's regular contribution to their Sunday laundry party day. Tuyen has tried to teach Billie how to make bánh pia, but her hands have no feel for dough and Tuyen has no patience with Billie's ineptitude. Her attempts leave Tuyen and her mother weak with laughter. Tuyen is devoted to Billie's mother.

Billie had no idea what a big sister might be, but she is starting to learn.

This morning, Tuyen made a double batch of bánh pia filled with its delicious sticky fruit paste. Scott, Henry and even gray wolf Doris are on their way over to meet baby Jean An.

Despite Billie's fears about Agent Orange, Jean An came into the world tiny and perfect, with all ten fingers and ten toes exactly where they needed to be. They all cried when she was born. Billie doesn't think about Jean An being Dan's baby. They haven't heard from Dan since the day he brought Tuyen. Jean An is *their* baby — Tuyen's, Billie's and her mother's.

Billie sets the camera on the tripod and screws in the shutter release cord.

"Look into here," she says, pointing to the lens and pantomiming to convey the meaning to Tuyen.

Her hands adjust the focus and the aperture. Through the viewfinder she sees her mother beam a huge smile at Tuyen, a smile that Tuyen then mirrors. Her mother points to the camera. Tuyen momentarily scowls. The camera is Billie's world, a world that Tuyen doesn't share.

The little bundle in Tuyen's arms makes soft sucking sounds. Tuyen's love transforms her.

Billie quickly places herself beside her mother and Tuyen. Her thumb hovers over the plunger of the shutter release cord.

"On three. One, two ..."

She looks deeply into the lens. She sees a convex image of three women and a baby girl, smiling.

A family. Her family. A future.

Click.

AUTHOR'S NOTE

There were many stages to the Vietnam War (known in Vietnam as the American War). From 1954 to 1975, the Communist government in North Vietnam fought to unite a divided country under one rule, while the South Vietnamese wanted to maintain an alliance with the United States and work toward a more democratic government. The conflict grew to become a focus of the Cold War between the Soviet Union, which supplied military aid to North Vietnam, and the United States, which supplied military aid to South Vietnam.

The Vietnam War was also the first mass media war. People witnessed daily the horrors of war on TV, radio and in print media. The troops who went over came back scarred, disfigured, with limbs blown off and minds traumatized. Across the world, people were horrified by the apocalyptic images and stories coming out of Vietnam.

Between 1964 and 1973, over two million American men were drafted into military service to fight in Vietnam. By the end of the war, 58,300 American armed forces were killed or reported missing in action. During this same time, over 50,000 draft evaders, deserters and women left the United States and moved to Canada.

Canada was not directly involved in the war. The Canadian government's position was that drafters had not broken any Canadian laws, so they were welcomed into the country. The majority settled in Toronto, Montreal and Vancouver. The Union of American Exiles on St. George Street in Toronto was a lifeline for refugees, and Mark Satin's *Manual for Draft-Age Immigrants to Canada* (House of Anansi) was passed from drafter to drafter. Many Canadians joined with Americans to protest lawfully against the war.

By 1968, a cultural shift was taking place. The protests became not just about ending the war, but also about questioning the role of the United States in global affairs. The war became a time to reckon with a colonial past, and for some, ending the war was not enough. It was time for a revolution. People went on hunger strikes. A few doused themselves in gasoline and self-immolated in a public attempt to bring attention to the atrocities that were being committed. And some turned to violence.

By the late 1960s and early 1970s, anti-war and anti-imperialist protest bombings and actions were almost daily occurrences in the United States and Canada. The Weather Underground became a violent offshoot of the SDS (Students for a Democratic Society). They bombed numerous buildings and institutions involved with the war effort. The Black Panthers were a political movement that confronted systemic police brutality against Black people with violent responses. In Quebec, the FLQ (*Front de libération du Québec*) bombed buildings connected to British imperialism and kidnapped government officials.

Although this is a work of fiction, it is based on true stories. As far as I know, there wasn't a plot to blow up the bridge outside St. Jacobs, Ontario. However, Agent Orange *was* being manufactured by the Uniroyal Chemical Company in Elmira and shipped via rail to the United States. There *was* a railway bridge built to connect Elmira to St. Jacobs and the main rail line. Articles on how to make your own bomb were readily available.

My mother and I moved from New York to Toronto in 1963. In 1968, when this story takes place, I was thirteen years old. My mother opened our house in Toronto to draft evaders. I was involved in anti-war protests and went to demonstrations in Queen's Park in Toronto armed with peanut butter and jam sandwiches to give out to hungry protesters. We lived around the corner from Rochdale College, where I went for movie nights and encounter group sessions. My mother and I bought a dilapidated farmhouse near Sebringville, Ontario, outside of Waterloo. It became a meeting place for artists, writers, and alternatively minded people. None of us picked up a gun or made a bomb. We thought that change could come through art, literature, gardening and love. We believed that peace in our time was possible.

It's a dream that I still believe in today.

ACKNOWLEDGMENTS

The late 1960s were not easy times, and people on both sides of the border were faced with many hard choices during those tumultuous years. I am deeply grateful to friends, neighbors and acquaintances for sharing their stories. In particular, I'd like to thank Steve Bryne, Annie Creighton, Molly Forsythe, Judith Fox-Lee, Jack Freeman, Mark Frutkin, Joe Hansgen, Terri Henderson, David Hines, Jim King, Charles Long, Ian Moffat, Michael Nault, Tom Neitman and Mary Rykov for their insights.

Thank you to Emme Reichert (Social Media Manager for Waterloo Central Railway) for filling me in on details about the rail line from Elmira to St. Jacobs, and to Brian Scott, who was incredibly generous and specific with his memories of the darkroom at Jarvis Collegiate Institute.

The Thomas Fisher Rare Book Library, University of Toronto, was a treasure trove of files, letters, posters and information. Thank you to Meghan Fitzpatrick and Tys Klumpenhouwer for helping me gain access to these documents.

Many thanks to Melissa Baumgart, who suggested Billie might live in Washington Heights and who guided me on my first journey north of 116th Street. Thank you also to

Frieda Wishinsky for additional information on Washington Heights in the 1960s.

Kathi Appelt, Martha Brockenbrough and Martine Leavitt were all early readers of the manuscript. Their incisive mentorship helped me to shape a grab bag of ideas into a novel.

I cannot say enough about my editor Shelley Tanaka. Her guidance, good humor and perseverance have changed my DNA as a writer. This book is a tribute to one of the best collaborative artistic relationships I have ever had. And I haven't gotten over the image of her visiting Rochdale in a Jaguar.

Tim Wynne-Jones, who has traveled on the journey with me since the days of Afros, caftans, beads and peace signs, is still my first and best reader. His wisdom and encouragement helped to keep me going through the dark days.

My mother, Laurie Lewis, taught me that you must do what you can to make the world a better place. She provided the framework for our lives in Toronto, which included the Underground Railroad, laundry parties and an open door for many people in need.

Thank you to Karen Li and Groundwood Books for their bravery and vision in publishing this book, and to the Canada Council for the Arts and the Ontario Arts Council for helping to sustain me and support my research. A full bibliography can be found on my website www.amandawestlewis.com. Any errors or omissions are entirely the fault of the author.

Amanda West Lewis has combined careers as a theater artist, calligrapher and writer. She has acted, directed, produced and written for theater, as well as founding The Ottawa Children's Theatre, a school dedicated to work by young people. Her calligraphic artwork has been exhibited in numerous shows, and she has written books on calligraphy and the development of writing. She is the author of nine books for young readers, including *These Are Not the Words*, a semi-autobiographical novel about Billie's early years growing up in New York City. Her books have been nominated for the Silver Birch Award, the Red Cedar Award and the Violet Downey IODE Award. She has an MFA in Writing for Children and Young Adults from Vermont College of Fine Arts.

Born in New York City, Amanda moved with her mother to Toronto, Canada, as a teenager. She now lives with her husband, writer Tim Wynne-Jones, in the woods near Perth, Ontario, where they raised their three children.